BECOMING JESTINA

Merrill J. Davies

Other Novels by Merrill J. Davies

The Welsh Harp (2012)

The Truth about Katie (2013)

Our Pebble in the Pond (2016)

© 2018

Published in the United States by Nurturing Faith Inc., Macon GA,
www.nurturingfaith.net.

Library of Congress Cataloging-in-Publication Data is available.

ISBN 978-1-63528-038-8

Cover images:
"Rosie the Riveter" | Public Domain
Jeremiah O'Brien Liberty Ship in San Francisco | © Mike Hofmann
Cover and interior design by Amy C. Cook.

PREFACE

Jane Tucker has been a good friend since we arrived in Rome, Georgia, in 1974 with two small children. She came to our house the next morning, volunteering to take care of our girls all day so we could unpack our belongings. We were soon able to take the girls to get their teeth cleaned with no resistance, since Jane (a dental hygienist) was their friend. Throughout their childhood, she often took them to the park or to McDonald's on Saturdays.

Five or six years ago I learned that Jane was a real "Rosie the Riveter," who had welded on Liberty Ships at Southeastern Shipyards in Savannah, Georgia. Since then I have accompanied Jane and and her other Rosie friends to presentations they do at schools, museums, and at Kennesaw State University. As I have listened to their stories, I have realized what a difference these women and others like them have made in women's lives, because they proved that women could do more than be secretaries, teachers, and nurses. The times demanded that they do things that women would ordinarily never do, and as a result, they eventually changed the way women have participated in the workplace.

All the stories I have heard from these women inspired me to write *Becoming Jestina*. Jane was an invaluable resource as I constructed the novel. Not only did I call her again and again to ask about details in scenarios I was trying to develop, but she also voluntarily brought me many helpful books and articles. In addition, we took a trip to Savannah together to visit city libraries and places Jane had visited during the war. In the process of doing research for the novel, I have learned much about World War II that I had never known before. I have included a selected list of works consulted at the end of the book. Since this is a work of fiction, I have not made footnotes on any particular details, but the reference list might prove helpful if the reader has questions.

I chose the name "Jestina" because it means "just and upright." Although this is a work of fiction, some of the incidents may include details from stories I have heard from Jane and her friends, as well as stories told in some of the books I have used. My hope is that this novel will honor my friend Jane Tucker, who celebrated her 90th birthday in 2017.

Dedication

To my friend Jane Tucker and all the other women who worked during World War II and changed the way women have participated in the workplace.

ACKNOWLEDGMENTS

As most authors know, there are always a host of people who support, encourage, give feedback, and make a book possible. There are a few, however, who always stand out—the ones who sacrifice their time to get a manuscript read so the writer can move on, those who step in when you need them at the last minute, and those who give honest feedback, even if it's not always positive. The ones who stand out in the creation of this novel are the following:

• Jane Tucker, of course, was the main inspiration for the book, but so much more. I could never have written the book without her help.

• Martha Heneisen, my good friend and fellow writer with a keen eye for my crazy mistakes, has read and given me feedback on the book at every stage of its development.

• Sharon McBrayer, a fellow English teacher in the past who is always ready to give feedback at any stage I ask for it, gave a final reading on very short notice.

• Dr. Sherrill Martin, retired professor at the University of North Carolina at Wilmington, took time from her own writing project to read the manuscript and write the back cover endorsement. As an added bonus, she did a close reading and found several editing errors.

• My husband Bill, who always gives unconditional support in every way possible, took time to read every word and gave honest feedback, and often gave me an encouraging word when I needed it most.

CHAPTER 1

The August heat and humidity had already arrived in Savannah by eight o'clock in the morning when the Thompsons got there. Jessie walked a little behind her mother and beside her older sister Cornelia as they entered the Southeastern Shipyards. Men worked and shouted obscenities at one another and hardly acknowledged the presence of the three women.

"Where do we go?" asked Jessie.

"I'm not sure," replied her mother. "They said to go to the administration building, but I don't see anything that looks like I thought it would be."

Jessie was still tired from the long sixteen-hour train ride from Alabama the day before. On August 2, 1943, Bernadette and the two girls, along with all their belongings, had boarded the train in Heflin, Alabama, to travel to Savannah, Georgia. Jessie usually enjoyed the train rides. She loved the wind blowing on her face as the train wound its way through the fields and forests and the little towns.

Boarding the train to Savannah had been a little different, however. "Look at all those young men headed out to war," observed Bernadette.

"Where?" inquired Jessie, having trouble keeping up with her mother and sister.

"On the train," responded her mother, pulling her suitcase behind her. "I don't think there are any seats available. It's filled with servicemen."

"You mean all the men on this train are going to war?" questioned Cornelia. "It must be really bad then."

"I'm afraid so," said Bernadette. It was Jessie's first glimpse of the reality of war.

When they finally got their suitcases on the train, they realized there was no place to sit and no place to put their luggage. "Let's just sit on our suitcases," suggested Jessie. And they did.

They changed trains in Atlanta, which was a little scary to Jessie. Most of her train rides had been to Birmingham. By the time they were on their way to Savannah, she felt more confident, but the change of trains in Atlanta wore on all of them. Again, they had to sit on their suitcases. The August heat was worse than she had imagined, and soon Jessie felt tired and sleepy.

"How long will it be until we get to Savannah?" she asked after what seemed to her like several hours.

"I'm not sure where we are, but the whole trip will take about sixteen hours," said her mother. "So I guess we have at least four or five more."

It was a long, hot, miserable day, and all of them were wondering if they had made a big mistake by the time they arrived at the massive train station in Savannah.

Bernadette's cousin, Chad Johnson, met them at the station and drove them to his house. He and his family made them feel welcome, but they all needed to rest. Bernadette and her daughters piled into one room and went to bed almost immediately.

Cornelia seemed happy about her mother's decision to come here to work. She had graduated from high school, so it was a good opportunity for her to get a job in the shipyards too. But Jessie had been looking forward to her final year in high school, and did not want a full-time job. Of course, no one listened to Jessie, and it was decided that they would all three go to work in Savannah. So here they were in this hot, stinky place looking for the administration building. Her mother looked around the shipyard.

"You girls stand right here and I'll go ask someone."

As Bernadette walked off, Jessie glanced around. The place smelled of dirt, grime, and sweaty bodies. The sounds of clanging, hammering, and other noises she'd never heard before filled her ears. She saw her mother talking to one of the workers, who was pointing down and to the left.

"Watch out, watch out!" several people shouted at once. Jessie turned around to see a huge gantry crane hoisting a big fabricated metal panel high in the air. It swung out of control and the eighty-five-foot crane fell over. Mama had said they'd only be here until the war was over, but Jessie wondered if they'd live that long.

"Do we have to do this?" asked Jessie when her mother returned to them.

"Of course," replied Cornelia. "It's exciting. Look at all those people working way up on top of those ships. I hope I get to work up there."

"But it's so hot out here. Mama, did you see that big crane that fell over? People could get killed—probably did," said Jessie, walking alongside her mother.

When they entered the building, they were in a huge room, like a big banquet hall. On the far end Jessie could see three doors going in to other rooms, and in between the doors were window openings where office workers were either dispensing papers or accepting papers from the long lines of people waiting to talk to them. Jessie, Cornelia, and their mother were directed to get in line to fill out applications. As they slowly progressed along with many other applicants, a lady pointed to Bernadette and said, "You get in this line."

The girls started after her, but the lady said, "No, not you."

"But we're together—" Jessie began.

Then the lady motioned to Jessie and said, "You go over there," and pointed across the room to a shorter line, leaving only Cornelia in the original line. Jessie looked around, trying to keep track of where her mother and sister were. Her mother caught her eye and mouthed, "Meet over there when you finish," pointing at the door where they had entered. Jessie nodded and continued in the line.

At the window where people were getting their application forms, she saw a sign that read, "BUY WAR BONDS," and below it was another: "GET ON THE BOND WAGON!" *What does that mean?*

When she finally got to the end of the line, the man gave her some papers to fill out. Name, address (*What was the Johnsons' house number?*), age, previous jobs, illnesses, and on and on. Jessie wished her mother, or at least Cornelia, were with her to help decide how to answer some of the questions.

When Jessie turned in the papers, she was sent to another room to wait to be called for an interview. It seemed like there were hundreds of people milling around carrying papers, asking questions. It was very confusing. She sat down in a chair and leaned her head back against the wall.

She wondered what her friends back home were doing. School would be starting in a few weeks, and she remembered the cheerleading skirt her aunt had made for her. It wasn't exactly like she'd asked for, but still she had looked forward to wearing it. School—was it over for her? She dozed briefly, but her head was at an uncomfortable angle.

After sitting there for what seemed like an hour, she heard someone call her name. Looking up, she saw a tall woman wearing a light blue blouse and navy slacks standing at a door across from her and realized that the woman had been the one calling her name. She got up and walked toward the woman.

"Are you Jestina Thompson?" the lady asked.

"Yes," Jessie answered.

"Okay. Come on in and have a seat," said the lady, indicating a chair across from a desk just inside the room.

"What kind of work have you done?" she asked.

"I worked in a five and dime store in Alabama where we lived before we came to Savannah," said Jessie. She looked down at the floor. "I know it's nothing like what I'll be doing here, but that's about all I've done."

"Did you apply for a job as a rod welder?"

"I guess. I don't know. I applied for a job. Is that what I'm supposed to do?"

The lady laughed, but it was more like a sneer. "Well, that's what we're hiring for today. If you want a job, that's it. Take it or leave it. I don't have time to haggle."

"Okay. I don't know how to weld though."

"You will when they get through with you. Do you want to work up on the ways or down in the yards?"

What is a "way"? Better not ask.

"I don't know. Do I have a choice?" Jessie watched the lady look down at the folder containing Jessie's application. She seemed to soften a little.

"Actually, you do. You don't have to work up on the ways. But we're always looking for daring young people who want to weld up on the overhead and the inner bottom of the Liberty Ships."

"Is it dangerous to work up there?"

"Well, yes, it is. How old are you? You look very young," observed the lady. Apparently, she had not looked closely at the details on the application.

"I'm sixteen," said Jessie. "But I'm strong, and my aunt says I'm smart."

"I'm sure you are both, but we'll just put 'no' for working up on the ways for now. If you decide you want to work up there after your training, there'll probably be opportunities."

It appeared to Jessie that the lady couldn't decide if she wanted to be tough or nice. She seemed to be trying to be tough, but Jessie thought maybe she really wanted to be kind.

Finally the interview was over. "Okay," said the lady. "You've got a job. Report to the welding school promptly Monday morning at eight to begin your six weeks of training as a rod welder. You'll be paid $1.20 an hour during training." Jessie did a double-take. A dollar twenty an hour? She'd be rich in no time! For a moment, she was almost glad they'd come.

Jessie got up and walked out and headed back through the throngs of people to the door where she had entered. Before she got to the door she saw Cornelia and her mother at the door waiting for her.

"How did it go?" asked her mother.

"I got the job," answered Jessie. "But I'm not sure I want it."

"I did too," said Cornelia. "I will be working up on the ways."

"Okay," said Bernadette. "So, it looks like all three of us will be working women beginning Monday morning."

"The lady I talked to said that the ways is a dangerous place to work," said Jessie. "I don't even know what they're talking about. What is a way?"

"The 'ways' is a wooden structure where they put the ships together, and then the ship slides down the structure into the water. That's the reason I volunteered to work there," said Cornelia, laughing. "It seems more exciting to me."

"You could get killed too," said Jessie.

"Jestina, don't say that," reprimanded their mother. She always called Jessie that when she was annoyed with her. "She'll be fine."

I don't know how welding will help me. I didn't like the way those old men looked at me either."

"But we're getting paid $1.20 an hour just for training," said Cornelia. "That's a whole lot more than you were making at the five and dime store—50 cents for a whole day on Saturday." Jessie had to admit she was excited about the money, but she dreaded the six weeks of training.

CHAPTER 2

Monday morning the Thompsons learned that Southeastern was launching one of the Liberty Ships at 8:30, but for the most part the ship launching was drawing little attention from the workers. There was the noise of hammering, clanging, and shouting as workers continued their usual tasks. Most of the workers were already sweaty and dirty, looking as though they had been there for hours. One of the employees had been assigned to take all the new trainees to the welding school.

During the first day they learned that they had to wear special clothing. They had already been told that they had to wear slacks, not skirts. Jessie had noticed that out in town, the folks looked at the girls funny and did not talk to them.

"There are several required components of the welder's attire," said the instructor. "The first is this leather suit," she noted, holding up the ugly gray thing as if it were a beautiful lady's gown. "Some of you won't have to wear the whole suit all the time, but you will need to pay attention to what tasks require it and which ones do not."

She went on to tell the class that in addition to the leather suit, they had to wear gloves, a helmet with a face protector, and a bandana. She proudly displayed examples of each of these items as she had done with the ugly suit. "As a welder, you must understand that your work clothes are about safety, not fashion," she emphasized, as if she doubted they understood.

"The bandana must be kept around your hair at all times," she explained, demonstrating how to tie it so their hair could not get caught in any of the machinery or go up in flames from the sparks during the welding process. Jessie remembered the time Cornelia's hair caught on fire at church during a candlelight service.

The woman continued explaining about everything, including the gloves and ugly high-topped shoes. As she demonstrated the use of each item, she would call up various new employees to help her show the class how to use them. One young girl who was very tiny held up her hands with the gloves on them. "These come all the way up to my elbows," she said.

"That's all right," said the instructor. Jessie thought the girl was hoping the lady would have smaller gloves for her, but she didn't. There didn't seem to be many exceptions. Jessie thought it a little excessive to spend a whole day's training on clothes, but what did she know?

The next day a mound of tools and equipment was piled in front of the class. There was a man giving the instructions, and he seemed to think the girls were all dense. He kept saying, "Do you understand me?" and "Do you have any questions?"

Most of the time Bernadette and her girls did not ask questions. Jessie wondered if Cornelia was paying attention. Once she saw her roll her eyes when the instructor kept repeating a statement about one of the tools. One girl asked something about the welding torch used by the burners.

He began by saying he was aware that girls probably knew nothing about all the mechanical stuff, and then ended by saying "You'd better be sure not to get distracted by some young man and burn yourself instead of the plate on the hull of the ship!"

Jessie clinched her fists and furrowed her brow. This was not the first time he had let them know that he did not really think they could do a "man's job." Noticing her reaction, her mother poked her in the ribs and said, "Shh."

Jessie looked at her mother, and then raised her hand. The instructor nodded at her and asked, "Yes, young lady, do you have a question?"

"Yes," responded Jessie. "I do."

"Well, spit it out, girl," he said. "What do you need explained again?"

"I don't need anything explained again. I need to know why you were so rude to that girl who asked about the welding torch. It was a very legitimate question that anyone could have asked." Cornelia and their mother were looking down at the floor.

The man looked down at the floor for a moment too and turned red. He hesitated as if trying to decide how to respond. "Well, I meant no harm. I was just trying to stress the importance of safety." He quickly went on to the next part of the lesson to prevent further discussion.

Walking back home that day, Bernadette said, "Jessie, you need to be careful what you say in that class. You know we have three more weeks of training before we become first class welders. You could get fired."

The girls both laughed. "I thought it was funny. I'm proud of you, little sister." Looking at her mother, Cornelia commented, "She just said what we all were thinking, Mama."

"I know, but we need the money right now, so don't mess it up." But a little smile played on their mother's lips.

The last three weeks went by faster because much of their training involved practicing the skills they had been taught.

One day when Jessie got home from work and finished with dinner, she suddenly felt her eyes begin to burn. She looked in the mirror and saw tears streaming down her face.

"Mama, look! What is wrong? My eyes are burning and all watery," she said.

"Oh, I bet you've got that 'welder's eye' they were telling us about," said Cornelia. "Remember. They even told us what to do, I think. What did they say?"

"They said to grate potatoes and make a sort of poultice to put on your eyes. It cools them down and makes them hurt less. I'll fix some for you," said Bernadette.

In a few minutes she returned and told Jessie to lie down and be still for a while with the treatment on her eyelids. After a few minutes, sure enough, she felt better. "Wow," she said. "It barely hurts at all now." In the back of her mind, though, she was not convinced that her eyes would not be damaged by this "welder's eye."

What if she went blind? Finishing school would not be an easy option if she was blind.

Every day it seemed there were new challenges and new tasks to master. Jessie was getting an education, but it was not the kind she had imagined for herself. Learning how to hold the welding equipment, how to avoid getting burned, and making sure to wear necessary safety garb were drilled into them during those weeks. Jessie couldn't help worrying about getting injured in some way. On the other hand, Cornelia didn't seem to worry at all.

"I can't wait to get started doing the real work instead of just practicing," said Cornelia one night after they got into bed. "This man in our class today said that women probably couldn't weld like the men. I'll show him!"

Jessie nodded. "I know. Did you notice the way he looked at that girl when she caught on quicker than he did about adjusting the flame? You could tell it made him mad to think a girl could beat him!"

Cornelia and Jessie did not always see things alike, but on this subject, they were in total agreement. Jessie admired her sister's willingness to take on a man's work with no reservations. Jessie herself was somewhat frightened by the job, but she was certainly willing to let anyone know that she believed women could do anything they set their mind to do.

The last week before they were awarded their certification as welders seemed the busiest. The Thompsons had been living with Chad Johnson and his wife Pat and their three children during their training as they saved money for a place of their own. Chad worked as one of the leadermen at Southeastern Shipyards, and he and his family rented a three-bedroom duplex in the Tatnall Homes area, built especially for Southeastern employees and within walking distance of the shipyards. Chad had insisted that Bernadette and the girls stay with his family until they could find something for themselves. The cousins were gracious, but the Thompsons knew it was difficult to make room for three extra people in a house that barely accommodated the family.

"When can we get a place of our own?" asked Jessie as they walked home one day.

"Soon," said her mother. "We might be able to look this weekend."

"I hope so. I hate not having a place just for us," she complained.

"I know, honey. It's hard on us, but it's even harder on them. I heard there were some openings here in the Tatnall section."

"Oh, I hope so," said Cornelia. "I like the Johnsons' place."

"Don't get your hopes up too much," cautioned Bernadette. "Everyone likes to live in Tatnall Homes because they are within walking distance of the ship-yards. Also, we may not be able to afford the rent."

When Jessie, Cornelia, and their mother received their welders' certificates on Friday, they were joyful, both because they had survived the training and because they would be able to look for their own place the next day.

Cornelia held her certificate out as they walked home, "Look," she said to anyone who would listen. "I am a certified welder!"

Jessie, however, did not feel excited. She was glad they had completed training of course, but she didn't necessarily like the idea of being a welder. It was just not something she was proud of.

Bernadette looked at Jessie. "You don't seem excited about your certificate. Are you not happy about our finishing the training?"

"Oh sure, I'm glad to be finished. It's just that I am not very excited about being a welder."

"I know, honey. But as I told you, this is just work during the war. We can make good money, and you can finish school afterwards and do something different. Right now they need women to help make these ships, so they're paying well."

CHAPTER 3

Friday night Bernadette told the Johnsons that she and the girls planned to look for a place to live on Saturday. Chad and his wife looked at each other and smiled.

"Well then, we may have some good news for you. We just heard that a duplex about three streets over from here has been vacated. You might be able to get it," said Chad.

"What's it like?" asked both girls at once.

"It has plastered walls, hardwood floors, kitchen and bathroom linoleum," answered Chad.

"And it has a gas stove and hot water heater, and coal-fired circulating heater. It's very much like this one," said Pat. "Except it's a two-bedroom instead of three."

Jessie didn't know anything about plastered walls and coal-fired circulating heaters, but it sounded nicer than anything she'd lived in before. Of course, in many ways she had loved living in Alabama with her grandmother, but it had been cramped and the house was old. "If it's available, when can we move?" she asked.

"It just depends," answered Chad. "Since the sign is up, I think it's probably already vacant, but I don't know."

The next morning Chad and his wife walked with the Thompsons to the house he had mentioned. They were unable to go inside because no one was there, but they walked on to the office where they could talk to the management of Tatnall Homes. Unfortunately, no one was there on Saturday either.

"Do you want me to check on that place for you Monday morning?" asked Pat.

"If you have time, that would help," said Bernadette.

Jessie and Cornelia moped the rest of the weekend, and couldn't wait until Monday evening to learn whether the house was still available and how much the rent was.

"I'm sorry," said Chad when they came home. "It was rented before they closed Friday. The sign was still there, but those houses are always snatched up as soon as they become available. It's that way with all these homes built just for employees. Maybe you should look up at Deptford Place. Those are not quite as popular as Tatnall, but they're still only about a quarter of a mile from work."

"Why are they not as popular?" asked Jessie. "Are they ugly or something?"

"Well, they are new, too—just opened in June. They are one-story and built of cinderblocks."

"What difference does that make?" asked Bernadette.

"The only thing I've heard is that you can't hang pictures on the walls," he said. "I don't think they're as large as these either."

"What else is there to look at?"

"Of course, there's Pine Gardens. Houses over there are a little more expensive, but it wouldn't hurt to look."

"At this point we just need to keep looking. Maybe something will turn up," said Bernadette resignedly. "Chad, I had hoped we could find something sooner than this."

"It's okay," Chad and his wife said at the same time.

"We know you're trying, and we really don't mind," continued Chad.

Pat laughed and added, "The kids love having you here. I think they're going to have a fit when you leave."

The Johnsons had three-year-old twin boys, John and Mack, and a daughter, Carol, who would soon be ten.

"You are very gracious, but surely we can find something by this weekend," said Bernadette. "I hate that Carol had to give up her room for all this time."

"Trust me—Carol is fine," said Chad. "I think she's enjoyed it."

When the Thompsons arrived home on Wednesday, Chad had some news. "A friend of mine over on Crescent Drive is leaving and has not told anyone yet. He is willing to let you look at his place and see if you like it."

"Great," said Bernadette. "Can we go now?"

"Yes. It's not far from here."

The Johnsons lived on Jones Street, so it wasn't a long walk to Crescent Drive. As they walked, Jessie observed the neat rows of buildings on each side of the street. They looked almost exactly alike, although some were a bit larger than others. Suddenly Cornelia pointed to the roof of one of the buildings. "Look!

Why do the buildings have such weird-looking roofs? They're all green and brown and mixed-up looking."

"Old Hitler's boys will have a hard time finding us!" said Chad. "They'll just think it's a bunch of trees and grass." He laughed.

"Does that really work?" asked Bernadette.

"Yeah. They tested it and it works. Almost every blade of grass, tree, or other natural feature has been put in there."

"But it's not all painted that way," said Jessie.

"No, but any exposed parts are, so from a plane, it would just blend in," said Chad.

"That's exciting," said Cornelia.

It's kinda' scary too, thought Jessie.

Most of the homes on Crescent Drive were duplexes. About a block after they turned onto the street, Chad walked up to one of them and knocked on the door. When the couple opened the door, Chad introduced the Thompsons to his friends and the wife invited them in. As she showed them around, the hardwood floors looked shiny and clean. In the kitchen Jessie noted the neatly arranged dishes above the kitchen cabinets. Remembering the dull floors and ancient-looking kitchen cabinets back home, she wondered what her grandmother would think. There was a white teakettle on the stove that looked like it had hardly been used! The place seemed like a playhouse to Jessie, or somewhere she might go for a vacation.

When they looked at the two bedrooms, Cornelia exclaimed, "Look Mama, you can have your own bedroom!" Back in Alabama, Bernadette had slept in the room with her mother, and the girls had shared a small attic room, but none of them had felt the luxury of a space like this. Jessie felt a twinge of sadness, thinking of her grandmother and the life she had left behind.

When Bernadette and Chad started talking to his friends about the details of their renting the duplex, Jessie and Cornelia went outside and walked around. By the time they left they had made a plan for the Thompsons to move in as soon as the house was vacant and there was time to clean it. It would take a few weeks, but at least they knew they had a place.

CHAPTER 4

It was mid-afternoon and Jessie stared at her torch as she welded the huge slab of steel, imagining what her friends back in Alabama might be doing. She held the torch steady and looked proudly at her work. Her friends were probably still at school, or maybe it was time for cheerleading practice. Suddenly she was aware of the voice of a coworker just down the line.

"We'll never get production recognition for being a star production crew," the man said. "We've got too many women on our crew."

"I know," answered his friend. "Look at them—girls!"

Jessie could see them out of the corner of her eye. The first man was one she had seen on the job before. He came in late some mornings, and he moved slowly and took long lunch breaks. She seethed inside, but she said nothing. When she finished her last job for the day, she hurried to catch up with one of her coworkers.

"I am furious!" she exclaimed. Her friend turned to her.

"Why?" she asked. "What are you talking about?"

"You remember that guy we watched the other day—the one who came in late and then moped along, slow as molasses?"

Jessie's friend nodded. "Yeah. I think his name was Walter. What about him?"

"Well, he was complaining about how our crew would never get recognized because it has too many women on the crew. As if we were the reason our crew has not been recognized! I say it is lazy people like him who slow our crew down."

"I guess he knows that many of the men will believe it's us though," said her friend.

"I guess so. I wish we could come up with a way to show him he's wrong," Jessie said.

That night Jessie could not stop thinking about the men who did not believe the women could work as fast or accomplish as much as the men could. She told her mother about what the men had said. "Do you think we can do just as much as they can?" she asked her mother.

"Of course, you can," answered her mother. "But you just need to ignore them. They're probably just jealous that you're making as much money as they are."

"But it's not fair, Mom," Jessie insisted. "Especially since that man is lazy himself. People like him are the ones who cause our crew not to be recognized. Why should we get the blame?"

"I know," sympathized Bernadette. "But you can't do anything about that. Most men around here think like that."

"Most men are wrong. And I intend to prove it."

"How?" asked her mother.

"I'm not sure, but I'll find a way," said Jessie. "Wait and see."

"Just be careful, honey. Don't get yourself into any trouble with other workers or your supervisors."

"I won't," Jessie promised.

It seemed like an easy thing to promise, but Jessie learned that sometimes things that seemed easy beforehand turned out not to be so easy. The next day Mr. Upchurch, the editor of the *Sou'Easter*, came out to the shipyards, which he did quite often, always looking for something unusual to write about in the little shipyard newsletter for employees.

He stopped by the big slab where Jessie was welding just after she had set the temperature control. "Looks like you've got a big job there, young lady," he commented.

"Yes, sir," she answered. She couldn't stop to talk. She had to stay focused to keep the flow of the metal going to the end of the seam. If she stopped or got distracted, it could cause her to mess it up. As she continued her work, she heard Mr. Upchurch speak to Walter, the guy who'd complained about the women workers.

A moment later she heard Walter say, "No, we haven't got any recognition yet. And we probably won't. Almost half of our crew is made up of women. Can you imagine that? And we're supposed to get these Liberty Ships out fast. How can we do that when we've got a bunch of sissies out here who don't even know how to weld?"

Jessie bit her tongue. Trying to stay focused was becoming harder. The heat was overwhelming, and her face was even hotter because of her anger. When she finished a strip she stopped for a moment and looked straight at Walter and Mr. Upchurch.

"It could be that we've just got a bunch of lazy men like you that's slowing us down!" she shouted. Both men looked her way.

"Now don't get all hot and bothered, little girlie," said Walter. "I'm just telling it like it is."

"The way it is, is that you came in a few minutes late three days this week, and you took a long lunch two of those days. And, you drag yourself around like a fat hog," she said.

She heard a footstep and looked around. There stood the leaderman. Jessie was in trouble. "That's enough. You two don't need to argue. My apologies, Mr. Upchurch. Please don't include this in your newsletter."

"I won't," said Mr. Upchurch. He grinned. "But it might make a good story."

As Mr. Upchurch left, Jessie's supervisor motioned for her to come over. "I'd like to see you in my office before you leave today," he said.

Jessie nodded. As she finished work that afternoon, she planned what she'd say to defend herself: *Walter was unfair. I had only told the truth about him. He should be getting fired, not me.*

Then she thought of her mother's words, and pondered how she could convince her supervisor that he should not fire her: *The heat had gotten to me. I will never do it again. I really liked working with Walter. He had just made me mad.*

By the end of the day, she didn't know what she'd do or say, but she knew she'd be in big trouble with her mother if she got fired, and she was pretty sure she would. What would she do all day now?

When quitting time came, she was exhausted, almost sick. She put away her equipment and headed for the leaderman's office. She walked slowly, still going over and over what she might say to convince her boss she was worthy of one more day on the job. She realized that she liked her work better than she had originally thought. Welding gave her a sense of putting things together in a way she wouldn't have thought possible. And for the most part, she liked her coworkers. But people like Walter made her a little crazy. She dreaded going into the office. The big doors creaked as she opened them, and then she had to go down a hall before entering the office. As she entered the office, the sight that met her eyes caused her to do a doubletake. There sat Walter! She stopped.

"Come on in and have a seat," said her supervisor.

"Thank you," she said as she settled herself into a chair as far away from Walter as possible.

"Seems like you two are not getting along too well," the supervisor commented.

"I guess not," Jessie said, remembering her desire to keep her job. She would wait a bit and see where this was going.

"I've had a chance to talk to Walter," said the supervisor. "And he has agreed to stop making public comments about women not doing their part. I would like to suggest that when you have problems with another employee you should bring these problems to me and not shout them out for everyone else to hear."

Jessie sat there and stared. He was not firing her. "Jessie?" he said. "Will you agree to this?"

"Uh—yes, of course. I'm sorry. It was just so hot out there, and I work hard and I get just as much done as anyone else. But yes, I promise to handle my problems better in the future."

"Thank you. You are both free to go." The leaderman stood, indicating that the meeting was finished. Jessie gathered her things and hurried out, hoping not to encounter Walter again. So, he had been called in too! That was encouraging.

She was not late enough getting home to arouse any suspicions, so neither her mother nor sister knew anything had happened. She was grateful for that and had practically forgotten about her encounter with her supervisor by the next afternoon. Unfortunately, not everyone had. On the way home one of her coworkers caught up with Jessie.

"Well, I see you're still on the job. I guess you didn't get fired after all," she said.

Jessie swallowed hard as her mother and sister jerked their heads around to hear what the girl was saying.

"No, everything is okay," she said, knowing that would not be the end of it.

As soon as the girl walked on ahead of them, Jessie's mother looked hard at her. "Okay, Jestina, what happened at work yesterday?"

Jessie walked on a few steps, trying to decide how to tell her mother and sister about her problem the day before.

"Oh, it was nothing much. Just a little argument with a man who was being ugly to me."

"It sounds like it might have been more than that. You know I can probably find out what really happened. You may as well tell me the whole story." Jessie knew her mother would dig until she got the facts, so she decided to just tell her the whole truth.

When she finished, she said, "Mama, I'm sorry. I just thought it was so unfair for someone who doesn't work as hard as I do to be acting as if the other girls and I were slowing our production down. It was just not right."

"I agree, Jessie, but you also have to realize that you can get in trouble when you don't control your tongue. Anyway, I'm glad you didn't get fired. That's something." Her mother did not pursue the subject, and neither did Cornelia. But that night Cornelia told Jessie she was right and she was glad her young sister was willing to stand up to people who did her wrong.

"Thanks, Cornelia," said Jessie. "But I just want to be back home with my friends finishing school. I hate it here."

"I guess I can see your point, but I like being in Savannah. It seems exciting here, and I couldn't make much money back home."

Jessie looked at Cornelia. Her big sister always loved excitement and adventure. It made sense that she would like this. "I just wish I could talk to Cassidy. I sent her a letter the day after we arrived and gave her Chad's address, but I have not heard from her. I can't imagine Cassidy working in a place like this. I'd just hate for her to see me now."

"Why?" asked Cornelia.

"Oh, I don't know. It just seems so—" Jessie searched her mind for the right word, but none came. Her friend Cassidy had seemed of a higher class of people than most of the workers here. She had moved in with her aunt and uncle, the Cohens, when she started high school. The Cohens owned a dress shop and were some of the most respected people in town.

"You mean you think Cassidy is above us welders?"

"Something like that," admitted Jessie.

"Well, let me tell you something, little sister. We are building ships, you and I. And these ships, they take supplies to the soldiers overseas. And because of that, we are helping win the war! Now I'm going to bed, but I don't care what your high-class friend thinks, because she can't get any better job than I have!" With that, Cornelia turned out the light and said no more.

CHAPTER 5

Jessie had thought about her sister's words often since that night, but she was still excited when Chad presented her with a letter from Cassidy the next evening. As anxious as she was to see what Cassidy said, she waited to open the letter until she was alone that evening so she could savor all the news from home. As soon as she finished dinner, she headed for her room while her mother and Cornelia finished cleaning up the kitchen. She took the letter from her pocket, unfolded it, and began to read:

Dear Jessie,

I am sorry I have not written until now. The store has been real busy these last few weeks, and I have been helping my aunt in the evenings at home also. I will try to fill you in on all the things going on here. First of all, they got a replacement for you on the cheerleading team. That makes me sad, but of course, you can't cheer for the team if you are living in Savannah. Also, you might be interested to know that Owen Doi and his parents have moved away. Someone said it was because of the way lots of people treated them here. I remember you telling me about the way some students treated Owen just after the bombing of Pearl Harbor, but I don't know what else may have happened. Anyway, I am not sure where they moved, but someone said they may have moved to Arizona. Well, that's about all I know to tell. I miss you and wish you were still here.

Your friend,
Cassidy

Jessie folded the letter and placed it back in the envelope. She sat quietly for a moment, remembering a scene at school in December 1941, the week after the bombing of Pearl Harbor:

"There he is! There's that Jap! I told you he'd be down on this hall."

Jessie turned as the group of boys came lumbering down the hall behind her and some other girls as they headed to class. She realized they were pointing at Owen Doi, who was just a little ahead of them. Owen was a quiet, shy tenth grader who was a year or so older than Jessie, although he didn't look it. He hugged his books close to him and looked really scared of the bigger boys taunting him. Jessie's face turned pale as the boys proceeded down the hall in pursuit of Owen, continuing to call him names.

"What are they talking about? Why are they pointing at him?" she asked her friends.

"Well, you know he is Japanese—both his parents are too," answered one of her friends.

The school and the whole town had been abuzz about the Japanese bombing of Pearl Harbor all week, but she didn't see what that had to do with Owen.

"Yes, but Owen hasn't done anything. Why are they picking on him?" she said. "He was born in the United States, and he and his parents are U.S. citizens just like we are, aren't they?"

"Well, yes, but my dad said you couldn't trust those Japs. They might act like they are Americans, but you just never know. Maybe they're spies or something," said Jessie's friend. "Look what they did at Pearl Harbor. Dropped a big old bomb and killed hundreds of people."

"Yeah, and they're not citizens 'just like we are' at all. They haven't been here all that long. My mom said she wasn't surprised. She said those Japs don't think like we do," said one of the other girls.

"Well, I still don't think those boys should bother Owen. He hasn't done anything. He's a nice boy. I've talked to him in my history class, and he's very polite and respectful," Jessie commented.

"Oh, well then, just go ahead and be a Jap lover if you want to, but you won't have many friends in this town," said one of the girls.

Jessie walked on to class, but throughout the day she kept thinking how scared Owen looked. She made it a point to speak to him every day when she saw him in class, but by the end of the week he was even quieter than usual, avoiding eye contact with those he knew.

During the two weeks before the Christmas break, Jessie had observed several instances when students would make a big show of walking on the other side of the hall when Owen approached, or just point at him and shout things such as

"Jap" or "traitor" or some other names to call attention to him. With each incident, Jessie could see that Owen was withdrawing more and more. She had been heartbroken. How could people be so cruel?

After one incident, where a student tripped Owen and made him fall, spilling his books all over the hallway floor, Jessie had reported it to one of her teachers. Surely her teachers would stop the harassment of her classmate. The teacher, a middle-aged science teacher, had looked at Jessie for a long moment.

"Why are you getting into this?" he asked. "He probably did something to them first."

"Well, I just feel sorry for Owen," she said. "They are doing this kind of thing all the time, calling him names, spitting at him, pushing him, and then today this boy just stuck his foot out and caused Owen to fall right in the hallway. It's unfair. Owen has never done anything to them."

"How do you know the boy meant to trip him? Maybe it was just an accident," the teacher asked.

"It wasn't an accident," avowed Jessie.

"Well, you really don't know that. Things like that happen all the time. I think you should just mind your own business and not worry so much about the Japs."

Leaving the teacher's room close to tears that day, Jessie had realized that the attitude toward her friend Owen was not limited to her classmates. She was not too surprised to learn the family had moved away when she read Cassidy's letter.

About that time Cornelia came into the room she and Jessie shared, and remarked, "I heard Chad say a letter came for you. Who was it from, and what did you learn?"

"It was from Cassidy. Everything is fine with her."

"Is that all?" asked Cornelia.

"Pretty much. They got someone to be a cheerleader in my place for this fall."

"Why did you want to do that anyway?" asked Cornelia, staring at her reflection in the mirror.

"Do what?"

"Be a cheerleader. You just don't seem like the type to be a cheerleader to me," said Cornelia.

"Oh, but I am," said Jessie, laughing. "You have a lot more friends, and get to know all the athletes. It's fun."

"Yeah. Well, I'd rather *be* an athlete," emphasized Cornelia. "That's why I ran track like our dad did. It's also the reason I like to work here. It may be hard work, but I'm accomplishing something."

"Like what?" asked Jessie.

"Like building ships," said Cornelia.

"You've said that before, but I just don't see it. I hate the heat, and the men all think I can't do anything as well as they can. Most of all, it's just boring work."

When they went to bed Jessie lay in the dark, thinking about Owen and his family moving to Arizona. She wondered what it felt like to be Owen. Was it anything like being a girl in a man's working world? She hoped Owen and his family would be treated well in Arizona.

CHAPTER 6

Finally, it was moving day! As much as Jessie hated to leave Alabama and move to Savannah, she had to admit that she was excited about her family's new home. Chad had been instrumental in helping them furnish the duplex with what they needed. One of Bernadette's coworkers had volunteered to use his truck to take some of the furniture over on the Saturday they were to move.

Jessie and Cornelia were responsible for packing all their clothes and other items into boxes provided by the Johnsons and loading them onto the truck. The girls then walked over to their new place, while Bernadette rode in the truck and the Johnsons stuffed their car with other supplies, dishes, and bedding.

As they approached the duplex, Jessie noticed a little girl of about five or six standing in the doorway of the other side of the duplex. She had black curly hair and huge dark eyes. As Jessie and Cornelia walked up to their side of the duplex, the little girl smiled shyly and then ran back inside.

Bernadette's coworker and Chad had carried in most of the heavy stuff by the time the girls got there, and they helped take the smaller items out of the Johnsons' car. Before long, everything was inside and the Thompsons were alone to sort out their belongings. Pat had packed some sandwiches for lunch, so Bernadette suggested they clean up the kitchen just enough to have lunch before they did anything else.

"That's a great idea," said Cornelia. "I'm starved."

"Why are we not surprised at that?" said Jessie.

They all laughed. Bernadette picked up the boxes on the table and deposited them on the floor, and retrieved the picnic basket with the peanut butter and jelly sandwiches. "Look," she exclaimed. "Pat also put apples in the basket—and a piece of her special chocolate cake!"

"Looks delicious," said Jessie. "I guess she's so glad to get rid of us that she wants to give us a grand send-off." They all agreed. It was the first time they had really been alone together for a while, and it was a moment to remember.

After lunch it was time to work on their bedrooms. The girls' room had twin beds, which Jessie and Cornelia positioned on either side of one of the windows. Near the other window they situated a small chest, and then put a small dresser with a mirror near the door at the foot of the beds. The room was small, but the girls were happy. It was better than they had been used to. They divided up the drawer space and chose their beds. Bernadette had purchased some almost-new bedding for them at a second-hand store.

Jessie sat on her bed once it was made up and looked around. It looked fantastic! She loved the looks of the shiny hardwood floors. But she realized they would feel cold on her bare feet this winter. Maybe they could find some rugs to put in front of their beds.

She walked into the bathroom and stood there looking at the bathtub, the toilet, and the sink. It was small and simple, but all she could think about was the way she had lived all her life. She could see herself going outside to the privy in the evening and taking a bath on Saturday in the zinc tub used for washing clothes. It would be filled with warm water and she could take an "all over" bath then. Her grandmother washed clothes on Monday after drawing water from the well, heating it in a big wash pot over a fire in the backyard. Looking at the bathroom now, it looked eloquent. She wondered what her grandmother would think about having an indoor toilet and a water heater!

"Jessie!" Her mother's voice startled her. "What is wrong with you? What were you thinking about?"

"Oh, I'm sorry—I didn't realize you were there," said Jessie.

"I spoke your name twice, and you just ignored me."

"I was just thinking about Grandma. I was wondering what she'd think about our indoor bathroom."

"She'd think it was grand, don't you think?" said Jessie's mother.

"Yes, I think so. She's always had to work so hard for everything," said Jessie.

When they finished with the bedrooms they went to the kitchen. The walls were painted white, and there were open shelves above the built-in cabinets. They put their plates, cups, and glasses on the shelves, and the silverware in the drawers beneath. When they got everything in place, Bernadette made a list of things they needed for cooking, eating, and cleaning. Amazingly, they had most of what they needed.

By three o'clock they had it all finished, and decided to take the streetcar down to the edge of town where there were a couple of stores. Bernadette looked around and smiled at their handiwork. "I think we'll have time to pick up a few essentials before the stores close."

As they were leaving the duplex, the little girl Jessie and Cornelia had seen earlier came out on the porch with her mother, and Jessie recognized her as one of the ladies who had been in their welding class. "Hello there," said the little girl's mother. "I'm Linda. I think I've seen you at the shipyards."

"I was thinking the same thing," said Jessie."

"Yes," said her mother. "I'm Bernadette, and these are my daughters—Cornelia and Jessie."

"This is my daughter Mary," said Linda.

Jessie bent down and spoke to the little girl. "Hi, Mary. I'm Jessie."

"Jessie?" asked Mary. "I thought Jessie was a boy's name."

"It can be," said Jessie. "Actually my real name is Jestina, but everyone—well, most everyone—calls me Jessie."

"Why?" asked Mary.

"Mary, don't ask so many questions." Linda looked at the Thompsons. "She's just at that age you know."

Mary looked perplexed. "I asked because I know this little boy and they call him Bill. His mother said his real name is William, but he hasn't grown into it yet. Are you going to grow into Jestina?" she asked.

"Maybe," said Jessie, laughing. "I guess it would be good if I did."

Linda smiled. "I'm glad you're here and look forward to getting to know all three of you."

"Same here," said the Thompsons. "We're headed downtown to pick up a few things, but we'll see you around."

After they left, Jessie said, "I haven't seen a man with Linda and her daughter. Have either of you?"

Bernadette and Cornelia shook their heads. "Her husband may be in the service," said Cornelia.

"Or she may not have one," said Bernadette. "I wonder if she's asking the same thing about us."

CHAPTER 7

Despite her excitement about their new living conditions, Jessie was often homesick for her school and friends and moped around in the evenings at home. She enjoyed the social life in Savannah, though, especially going to the movies at the Lucas Theater downtown and to dances with Cornelia and her friends. Knowing that slacks were frowned upon in town, the girls would go home after work and shower as quickly as possible before heading out for an evening of fun.

"Be careful when you go out to those dances and movies. You can't trust a man," warned Bernadette.

"Why not?" asked Jessie.

"You just can't," said her mother. Bernadette often warned them of the dangers of being out late at night. Jessie wasn't sure why, except that she still seemed bitter about her relationship with their father. She never really talked about it, though, so the girls didn't know what had happened between them. They had seen their dad only a few times since he left.

They all worked long days in the hot summer heat that extended into late fall in 1943. Most of the eligible men were away in the war, but the girls were lucky to have many young soldiers in the Army Air Corps at nearby Hunter Air Base and Fort Stewart. They were always looking for young girls to accompany them to movies and dances. Coming from all over the United States, they were looking for a good time every night of the week. Jessie was fortunate to have an older sister to accompany her, and her mother trusted Cornelia to bring her home safely after the movie or dance.

Her sister's "supervision" came at a cost to Jessie, however. Cornelia always had her first choice of a date. Most of the time it was no problem, as they didn't usually know any of the guys, and Jessie didn't mind letting Cornelia choose first.

Often some of the older shipyard workers would bring food and beverages for the dances at the base. Bernadette had agreed to help at one dance, and all the girls were going. Cornelia's friend had met some guys the night before and had agreed to dance with one of them and to bring Cornelia and Jessie for the other two guys. The three soldiers arrived a little early.

Cornelia's friend pointed toward the door. "The one in front is my date. The other two are yours. I think their names are Al and Robert, but I don't remember which one is which."

Cornelia immediately pointed to the taller of the two. "I'm taking him because he's taller. Jessie, you get the one in the baseball cap."

Jessie guessed that he might be an athlete, maybe even a baseball player. She could tell him about the Southeastern baseball team's game at Grayson Stadium Saturday. Cornelia's date introduced himself as Robert. The one in the baseball cap was Al.

Jessie looked at him, noticing that he was indeed a good bit shorter than his friend Robert. "I'm Jestina, but you can call me Jessie. Everyone else does," she said.

"Why would I want to do that? I like Jestina," he said. "It's Welsh. It means 'just and upright' like the masculine name Justin. So I think I'll call you Jestina."

"I don't know why most people call me Jessie. Maybe it's like my little next-door neighbor said. Maybe I haven't 'grown into' my name yet," she said.

As soon as introductions were made, Cornelia and her friend and their dates seemed to disappear, leaving Jessie and Al to fend for themselves.

Al Donaldson was the type of guy who seemed to work at making others feel good about themselves. Jessie liked him instantly. Just as they were about to begin the first dance, two things happened: Jessie noticed that the other two girls were staring at her from the other side of the room, and Al removed his baseball cap.

Jessie swallowed hard and tried not to stare. Al had no hair. *No hair.* Not a short haircut like all the other soldiers, but *no hair.* He was completely bald. Fortunately, Al was used to this reaction.

As soon as he saw her face, he said, "I'm sorry. I shouldn't have worn that stupid ball cap. I had it on because I was out in the sun, and then I thought I'd just keep it on until I met the girl I was to dance with, but now I see it was a foolish idea."

"No, I'm sorry," Jessie said. "I was the one who was gawking. I guess I was just—well, surprised."

"Of course you were. Don't feel badly. People expect one to have hair," he said, smiling.

She relaxed. "So, have you always been bald?"

"No, but flying those B-17 bombers creates a lot of stress I guess. I don't know, but that's what the doctors say. Maybe it'll grow back—and maybe not, since I'll have to go again in a few weeks." He said it casually, as if it were no big deal.

During their conversation they just naturally sat down on the sidelines and continued talking as the music began to play. "So, Jestina Thompson, do you want to dance with a bald man?"

"Of course!" she said. "If that's an invitation?"

"It sure is!" said Al, grinning. "I'm a pretty good dancer, too—even if I don't have hair."

By the end of the evening Jessie had learned that Al had flown more than thirty missions on the B-17 and that he would likely be flying more. No wonder he had symptoms of stress! When the dance was over and they were on their way home, Cornelia said, "I'm sorry, Jessie—I didn't know!" She laughed.

"What do you mean?" said Jessie. "Why are you sorry?"

"I didn't know he was bald. I swear," said Cornelia.

Jessie realized that she had already forgotten about Al's hair—or lack of it. He was such a nice person that she had completely forgotten about it.

"Look, Cornelia, I had the best time I've had since we've been in Savannah. You don't need to apologize. He is a really great guy—hair or no hair." For the first time Jessie realized that one can really make a bad mistake by judging someone by his looks. She promised to always remember that.

The following week Jessie had another chance to remember her experience that night. She had noticed that there were a good many black workers at Southeastern Shipyards. Every day when she came to work she saw one young black man working near the gate. One day she heard him say something about playing baseball and assumed he was on Southeastern's team. She planned to go to a game that weekend, so she mentioned it to one of her coworkers.

"Oh, and that guy right over there is on the team," said Jessie.

"Which one?" said her friend.

"The black one. I heard him say so this morning when I came in."

"Well, he's not on the Southeastern baseball team," said her friend. "He couldn't be."

"Why?"

"Because he's black. Are you crazy?"

"Well, I thought—you know—we all work together in here," said Jessie.

"No, we don't. They work here, but it's not the same. Do you see any of them in management, or even welding?"

"No," admitted Jessie. "But the advertisements for workers—it sounds like we're all the same in here."

"Don't kid yourself. We're not the same. They do have a team, but it's sponsored by the Colored Athletic Association, not the Southeastern Athletic Association. Just watch the *Sou'Easter*. You'll not see much about their team in it, or in any of the local newspapers in Savannah."

"I think that's unfair. Why wouldn't they just all play on one Southeastern team? I think if we're all employees here, then it doesn't make sense to have two different teams. It'd probably be a much better team," said Jessie.

"It doesn't matter what you think, Jessie. That's just the way it is. So get used to it," said her friend.

Jessie fumed on her way home that day. Growing up in Alabama, she had never questioned the way things were much, but now she realized that it was the same situation as Owen had. People were judged by the color of their skin, their nationality, or some outward appearance.

Al was on leave for two weeks, and since he had no close relatives in Georgia, he stayed on base. During those days Jessie saw him several times. If she had been older, she might have considered Al a good candidate for marriage, but Jessie saw him as a dear friend. They talked about all sorts of things—their families, their beliefs, and their educational goals. Jessie even told him about Owen and how students had treated him.

"Knowing what it's like to be shunned, I can feel for Owen," said Al. "I've been shunned a lot during my life, even before the hair problem. I just never seemed to fit in with others. Since my father died when I was a kid, I had to be more mature and help Mom with my three younger sisters, so I didn't think the way most of my classmates did."

"I don't guess I'd ever felt 'shunned' until I stood up for Owen," said Jessie. "I did feel a little out of place in high school. I didn't have many friends who thought beyond graduation, and I always wanted to go to college."

"You should keep thinking that way," said Al. "You are smart. There's no reason girls shouldn't do whatever they want to. And speaking of Owen, just remember that these are unusual times. People are afraid of the Japanese, and fear causes us to act in a different way sometimes. I understand, though, that your friend was being treated unfairly."

"When I saw the way people treated Owen because he was Japanese, I began to have more of a purpose in getting an education. And another thing I have thought about recently is the way the black folks are treated. I'd like to help people who are mistreated. I don't know what I could do, but surely there is something."

"You'll find a way," Al said. "Just keep learning. When this war is over, I plan to go back to school too, but I have no idea what I want to study."

When Al's leave was over and he returned to duty, Jessie missed him. But they promised to write to each other. She believed she had indeed found a life-long friend.

Thinking of her friendship with Al that night, Jessie recalled the weekend her mother had taken her and her sister to Birmingham to see *Casablanca*. Would she and Al be like Ilsa and Rick? Probably not. She seemed to remember every detail of her trip to see the movie. It was still dark when Bernadette came into the girls' room on a wintry Saturday morning to tell them it was time to get up—even earlier than they usually got up for school. At first Jessie thought it was another school day, and then she remembered. As it dawned on her that it was the "big day" she had been waiting for, her mother shook Cornelia's shoulder.

"Wake up! Rise and shine! The train leaves for Birmingham at 7:30 this morning, and it will not wait for us."

Both girls struggled out of bed and began to get dressed and check the suitcase they had packed the night before.

Cornelia was always hungry. "What's for breakfast?" she wanted to know.

"I've made biscuits, and we have some apple jelly."

"Great. I'm starved."

Jessie just wanted to get on the way to the train station. Finally they were out the door and making the fifteen-minute walk before boarding the train. They arrived at the station a bit early, and Bernadette asked the attendant where they should wait, telling him that they already had their tickets.

"How long does it take to get there?" asked Cornelia.

"About four hours," said Bernadette.

"Four hours? Did you bring anything to eat?"

"As a matter of fact, I did," said her mother. "I brought each of you another biscuit with jelly. Oh, and I also found a piece of candy for each of you."

They boarded the train promptly at 7:30 a.m. and settled down for the long ride. The biscuits were gone before the first hour had passed, but their mother made the girls wait until the end of the third hour before she gave them their candy. Soon afterward they pulled into the train station in Birmingham and saw Bernadette's cousin waiting for them.

Casablanca! Jessie couldn't believe they were going to see the movie just after it came to Birmingham! She had read in a magazine all about the story when it was made into a movie last year. But knowing how long it would take to get to their hometown, she had not thought about getting to see it this soon.

The movie was a very timely one because of the Allied invasion of North Africa, the location of Casablanca. It was a love story too. Warner Brothers promised adventure, intrigue, and romance. She couldn't keep all the details straight, but she did remember that Humphrey Bogart and Ingrid Bergman were the stars. Although some of Jesse's friends said it sounded boring, Cassidy was just as excited as she was about the Thompsons' trip to Birmingham to see it.

As they entered the theater, Cornelia looked at Jessie. "Now tell me again what this is all about." Although she was excited to be there, Cornelia just enjoyed the trip and the idea that they were going to a newly released movie. She had not read much about the story.

Jessie began by saying, "First of all, it is supposed to have happened in Casablanca, a city in Morocco, which is in North Africa. Humphrey Bogart plays Rick Blaine, who is an expatriate who runs an American café—I think. Anyway, it's all very complicated and I can't remember much of it. Part of it, though, is that it's a love story and Ingrid Bergman stars as Ilsa Lund, a former girlfriend of this Rick Blaine."

"Okay. That's enough," said Cornelia. "Sounds good to me."

That Saturday night the movie drew a big crowd. The theater was packed, and excited voices discussed war-time politics, some of them arguing about actions by the President and many of them talking about the bombing of Pearl Harbor. Bernadette led the girls toward the door and presented their tickets before entering the darkened theater. They made their way down about halfway and sat in the middle section. It was only a few minutes before the news came on, informing them of what was happening on the battlefields. As usual, family members looked closely each time a news flash had pictures of a place their loved one might be. Then the advertisements started, encouraging viewers to buy war bonds. Admonitions to "Buy more bonds—get on the bond wagon!" filled the theater.

Jessie was intrigued by the whole movie—even the parts she didn't quite understand. But she was most fascinated by the love story of Rick and Ilsa. At times she was afraid, and at the end she almost wept, but she was swept away by the romance of the two. Oh, to have a love like theirs! She couldn't wait to tell Cassidy all about Humphrey Bogart and Ingrid Bergman. Cassidy had said that Humphrey Bogart was her favorite actor.

As Jessie thought of her friendship with Al and looked back on the weekend she'd seen *Casablanca*, it seemed like a long time ago, but it had only been a few months. But her world had changed dramatically in that short time.

CHAPTER 8

Jessie and her mother usually took their lunches to work and did not make the long walk down to the cafeteria close to the administration building. With only about thirty minutes to eat, it was easier to pack a sandwich and stay close by the work area. Because many of the black workers were not allowed to eat in the cafeteria, most of them brought their lunches too.

One day when Jessie got there before her mother, she opened her lunch box and suddenly heard one of the black girls shout, "Look out! Watch for the seagull!" Jessie instinctively closed her lunch box just as she saw the seagull going for it.

"Thank you," Jessie called.

"You are welcome," said the girl. "Yesterday, one grabbed half my sandwich and got away with it before I realized what had happened!" It's safer up here under the ways. I usually hide up here."

Jessie walked over to where the girl was eating her lunch. "I'm Jessie," she said. "Where do you work?"

"I work up on No. 6 slab. My name is Samantha, but everyone calls me Sam."

"What do you do? Are you a welder?" asked Jessie.

"Oh no! We are not allowed to do those kinds of jobs. I wish I could though," said Samantha.

"But why are you not allowed to weld?" asked Jessie.

"Look at me, Jessie. What color is my skin? Obviously you haven't lived around here long."

Jessie was embarrassed. "Well, I haven't lived in Savannah long, but I should have known because it would have been the same in the small Alabama town where I lived before."

She had not thought about it. After that day she began to notice more about the way black people were treated than she had before. Even though they were almost always nearby at lunch time, she noticed that she seldom saw any of the white employees talking to them and she saw some of her friends glaring at her when she did. Nevertheless, Jessie continued to learn about Sam's life growing up in East Savannah. Sam told her that she wanted to continue her education when the war was over, just as Jessie did.

About a month after her first conversation with Sam, Jessie was transferred to work on the slab where Sam was the helper. Since there was little time for talk during work time, they seldom spoke, but one day Sam was helping someone near Jessie. Jessie was wearing goggles and couldn't see very much around her. Suddenly Sam shouted, "Jessie, get down!" and shoved her down. A huge steel plate had barely missed her when the gantry had moved too fast. When Jessie realized what had happened, she thanked Sam profusely. "I think you just saved my life!" she told her.

After that Jessie and Sam usually talked during lunch. They learned that their lives were not that different except for the color of their skin and the resulting discrimination Sam experienced. They both loved books and school, and regretted having their schooling interrupted, but Sam accepted it a little better than Jessie did. Sam's interest, however, was in science. She loved science and wanted to get into the field of medicine.

"It's hard enough for women to get into medical school though," she said to Jessie one day, "and probably impossible for a black woman."

"So you want to be a doctor?" asked Jessie.

"My mother died of cancer when I was ten," she said. "I said then that if there was any way I could become a doctor and learn ways to treat cancer, I wanted to do that in her honor."

"Oh, I hope you can," said Jessie. "I could never be a doctor myself, but I certainly hope it will be possible for you. I am so sorry about your mother."

Sam looked at her unlikely friend. "What do you want to study?"

"I'm not sure. I've thought about law, but like medical school, many law schools do not accept women. So I don't know."

Sam laughed. "For two girls working in a shipyard, we sure have big goals, don't we?"

"I guess we can dream big," said Jessie. "It's what keeps me going, working in this awful place. Don't you just hate it?"

"In a way I do, but then I'm making a lot of money compared to what I could make anywhere else, so maybe it's a good thing that way."

"You could make even more if they would let you train to be a welder," said Jessie. "I don't understand why they won't let you weld. You are just as capable of doing it as I am, or anyone else."

"They won't though. Look around. Do you see anyone of my color doing a skilled job? It's not allowed." Sam laughed. "My brother said that some of our kind did get to be welders in Brunswick—men, of course, not women. But anyway, when he told that, some of the workers heard about it and somehow people here got out a rumor that it would happen here and it would take the women welders' jobs. A bunch of people got really mad. Of course it didn't happen—and probably never will."

"But if your folks are already skilled in something, wouldn't they let them work in a skilled position? It seems like they'd need skilled workers."

"My cousin is a diesel mechanic. He put that on his application. When he turned it in, the man looked at it and then tore it up. He told my cousin to put 'laborer' on the application."

"That just seems so unfair," said Jessie. Sam just sighed.

The more Jessie thought about the matter, the more unfair it seemed that a person as smart as Sam had no chance of becoming a welder just because of the color of her skin. One day when Jessie went to deliver a message to her supervisor, she said, "I have a friend who would make a good welder. Do you need any more good welders?"

"We always need good welders," he responded. "What is she doing now? Is she an employee?"

"Yes, she works here. Her name is Samantha or 'Sam.' She is a helper on Number 6 slab."

"You mean the black girl?" he asked.

"Yes."

"Surely you know we can't train her as a welder," he said.

"Why not?"

"We just can't, and I would advise you not to be talking so much to that girl," he said. He walked off. The conversation was over.

When she told her mother about the discussion, her mother reacted as usual. "Just be careful what you say," she said. "We need these jobs."

Jessie did not try to discuss it with her mother again. But she did not forget the conversation with her supervisor, and she did not follow his advice not to talk to Sam.

CHAPTER 9

By November of that year it was getting cold, or so Jessie thought. Her friend and coworker from Illinois kept saying it was nothing like it had been back there, but Jessie thought it was getting cold. She added on a layer of "long handles" under her work clothes.

It was true that by Chicago's standards, Savannah's winters were probably not bitter cold, but that winter was colder than usual. One morning Jessie begged her mother to let her stay home. It was cold and windy and she hated the thought of working outside on those steel slabs. Her mother didn't relent though, and they wrapped up and made their way down to the shipyard.

When they entered the gate and checked in for work, even the gatekeepers seemed grim and cold. Ice had formed on the steel decks, and people were slipping and sliding, hardly able to get where they were going. By the time Jessie got to her work site, the supervisor told them they had decided to delay starting work until later in the morning, hoping the ice would melt off once the sun came up. They were told to go down to the auditorium of the administration building, and they would be told when to report back.

Sure enough, about ten o'clock that morning they were told to return to work. Indeed the ice had melted away, but Jessie was still freezing. When she had to sit down on the steel slab it was like sitting on ice. Fortunately she found a piece of cardboard and sat on it. That helped, but it was still cold.

That night Jessie was unusually tired and sleepy. As soon as dinner was finished, she told Cornelia and her mother that she was going to bed.

"Oh no you don't," said Cornelia. "It's your turn to do the dishes. You're not getting out of it either. We're all tired." Her mother agreed and Jessie did the dishes, but she felt unusually exhausted by the time she finished.

"Okay, the dishes are done and I'm going to bed," she said, as she headed for her room.

As she walked down the hall, she heard Cornelia say, "I guess she was really tired."

She fell asleep almost immediately, but about two o'clock in the morning she awoke burning up with fever. Cornelia woke their mother up when she saw how sick Jessie seemed. Bernadette brought a cold wash cloth and washed her face with it. Jessie sat up, trying to shake the feeling that the room was spinning around and around. Her throat was throbbing. After several cold cloths were applied to her face and arms, Jessie's fever seemed to go down a bit, and she told Cornelia and her mother that she thought she could go back to sleep.

When she awoke the next morning, however, she still felt weak and feverish. Her mother decided she should stay home from work that day, but Bernadette and Cornelia went on to the shipyard. Jessie slept most of the morning, ate a sandwich at lunch, and took another nap. By the time Cornelia and her mother returned that evening, Jessie felt a little better. The next morning she decided she was able to return to work.

When she arrived at the shipyard she was still a little shaky, but she checked in and went to her work site as usual. When she was issued her equipment, she thought they felt rather heavy, but she started her work anyway. She made it through the morning and met her mother for lunch.

"Are you all right?" asked Bernadette. "You look pale."

"I'm okay. I just wish I could take a nap."

"Well, you know you can't nap on the job," said her mother. "I don't know exactly what your supervisor does, but they've been really cracking down on loafing on the job in a lot of areas. Some of them play all sorts of pranks on people who are caught sleeping on the job."

"I wouldn't do that," said Jessie. "I just said I would like to take a nap. I am not planning to take one."

"If you get to feeling real bad, though, tell someone, and go to the infirmary," said her mother. "You really look like you don't feel well."

"Okay," she said, as she closed her lunch box and headed back to work.

When she returned to her slab to work, she was glad she had to work at the bottom of the panel, and could get a piece of cardboard and sit down for a bit. As she began welding, she felt faint for a moment and took off her goggles and laid her equipment beside her. *If I could just lean my head against the panel for a moment*, she thought.

The next thing she knew, she heard her coworker saying, "I think she's sick, sir. I don't think she's just sleeping on the job." She opened her eyes to see her coworker and her supervisor standing over her.

"What's wrong? Are you sick?" her supervisor asked.

"I guess I am. I had a sore throat and fever yesterday and stayed home, but I thought I was well enough to come back. I don't know what happened. I just thought if I could lean my head up against the panel a moment—"

"I think we'd better get you over to the infirmary," he said. "Would you go with us?" he asked her coworker.

Her friend accompanied them to the infirmary, where she waited for a few minutes to see the doctor. He was an older man who seemed compassionate and kind. After asking Jessie a few questions, he examined her, looking at her ears and throat.

"You probably should have stayed home another day or so, young lady," said the doctor. "Your throat looks pretty bad, and you don't need to be working today. I'm going to give you some of these little pills. They are new, but they are supposed to help a lot. Take two each day. But you probably should stay home tomorrow and maybe the next day, depending on how you feel."

Her friend spoke up for the first time. "Her mother and sister work here, and they usually go home together. Should I notify them that you're sending her home?"

"You could, or since it's afternoon, Miss Thompson, you can just lie down on that cot over there until they get off from work, and go home with your family."

"I think that would be better," said Jessie. "Would you tell my mother where I am?" she asked her friend.

Jessie fell back asleep on the cot. Soon she heard her mother talking to the doctor. Jessie opened her eyes and looked at her mother.

"I told her she didn't look good at lunch," said Bernadette.

"I've told her to stay home tomorrow, and then see how she feels the next day. I have given her some pills that should work quickly, but she's a pretty sick young lady," said the doctor.

Jessie went straight to bed when they got home, and stayed there. She was not hungry at dinnertime. All she wanted to do was sleep. During the night she dreamed she was back home in Alabama. Her grandmother was feeding her chicken soup and washing her face with a cold cloth. It seemed so real that when she awoke the next morning, she asked Cornelia if their grandmother had been there. Of course, Cornelia said no.

"But she was talking to me and giving me soup," said Jessie.

"I think you were delirious," said Cornelia, laughing. "You were acting really weird, and Mama came in and washed your face with a cloth and finally you calmed down."

"It was so real. I could hear Grandma's voice, and she was washing my face with a cold wash cloth."

"Trust me, it was Mama," said Cornelia.

Cornelia and Bernadette left for work after giving Jessie exact instructions about resting and taking her medicine during the day.

It was the longest day Jessie had experienced in a long time, but it gave her time to do a lot of thinking and reflecting on her life in Savannah. As she wandered around the house that day, she picked up the one thing her grandmother had insisted she take with her: her Bible. She read a few verses and thought back to her life in Alabama.

Her grandmother was the one who always took her to Sunday School and church. She loved to go with Grandma. Everyone always spoke to her and told her how pretty she was, and most of her friends were there. Jessie's mother hardly ever went with them, and Cornelia didn't go often either once she got in high school, but Jessie loved going. It seemed like the one place she felt safe and happy.

As she read some familiar scripture passages, she decided that she ought to go to church in Savannah on her Sundays off. She remembered seeing a sign on a church that read "First Baptist Church," and she thought she could find it again.

By the next day Jessie felt much better, and although she still felt a little weak, her family decided it would be okay for her to return to work.

CHAPTER 10

On Sunday morning Jessie told her mother and sister that she planned to visit the Sunday School at First Baptist Church in Savannah.

"I don't know about that," said Bernadette. "You've been sick most of the week, and that's a big undertaking."

"No it's not," said Jessie. "I know how to get there. Remember, we walked right past it the last time we went downtown."

"Where is it?"

"It's on the corner of Bull Street and McDonough," said Jessie. "It's right downtown."

"Does the streetcar go close to the church?" asked her mother.

"It goes close, but the city bus goes closer," said Jessie. "I think the bus actually goes within about a block of the church."

"Oh, I see you've been asking around already," said her mother.

"In fact I have," Jessie answered.

"Well, okay then. Just be careful," said Bernadette. She looked at Cornelia. "Do you want to go with her?"

"Not really. I'd rather stay here and listen to the radio."

Having made several trips downtown with her mother and sister, Jessie felt confident that she could go there by herself, and the bus stop wasn't far from their house. Even so, she was a little nervous when she stepped on the bus all alone. The only other passengers were three little black girls and their mother in the back of the bus. They were all dressed up in their Sunday clothes and sat quietly, not moving or talking.

After several stops an older man in a suit boarded the bus. Carrying a Bible, he took a seat across from Jessie. He nodded at her and then opened his Bible and read for a bit before the next stop, where the woman and children got off and two women got on. The two women were talking to one another and paid no attention to Jessie or the older man. As they got further downtown, the man looked at Jessie and inquired, "Are you going to church this morning, young lady?"

"I am going to First Baptist Church at the corner of Bull and McDonough, but I'm not sure where to get off."

"Oh, that's where I go, so you can just get off where I do," he said. "It's just a block from the bus stop. I can show you where to go for Sunday School. The young people's class is on the way to mine."

"Thank you," she said. She relaxed a little at the thought of not having to figure out how to get to the church, and she hadn't even considered the fact that she had no idea where the class met in the building.

Coming down Whittaker Street, Jessie thought they were getting close to where the church was. When the older man got off, she followed him down the street. Almost as soon as they got off, Jessie saw the big limestone columns of the church. Instead of going in the front entrance, the gentleman headed down the side and into another part of the building. As they started down the hall, he stopped briefly and pointed down the hall to his left.

"You'll go right down there to the second door on the right," he said. "The teacher should already be there."

He started on down the hall, and then turned around. "Do you need help finding your way back to the bus stop? It usually is coming in about the time I get out of church and back to the stop, maybe fifteen minutes after church."

"I think I can find my way, but thanks. I guess I'll see you on the bus."

Something about walking down the hall toward the classroom made Jessie a little uncomfortable. Why didn't she make an effort to get Cornelia to come too? Or a friend maybe? Her mother and sister had never seemed interested in going to church back in Alabama, and she had not thought much about including them, but now she was getting the jitters. By the time she entered the room it looked as if most of the young ladies were already there, and the teacher was about to begin. She looked to be about middle age and was dressed all fancy. In fact, all the girls looked much better dressed than Jessie.

The teacher turned toward Jessie and looked at her just a little too long. Jessie's face felt hot, like she did not belong, but she was not sure why.

"Oh, we have a visitor," said the lady.

Jessie didn't know what to say, so she said nothing.

"What is your name?" asked the teacher.

"I'm Jessie Thompson," she stammered.

"Well, have a seat, Jessie. We are *delighted* to have you," the teacher said, exaggerating the word "delighted." She did not seem delighted, and Jessie did not feel comfortable at all. But she sat down on the end of one of the rows of seats beside one of the girls.

The girl beside her asked Jessie if she was new in Savannah, and Jessie shook her head. Then the teacher asked her if she was in school in Savannah.

"No. I work over at the shipyards," Jessie said.

Suddenly a hush came over the room, and several girls looked back at her. It was as if she had said she was a thief or a murderer—or maybe a hooker. The teacher quickly got out her Bible and began to teach the lesson. Ironically, it was the one about Jesus eating with sinners. The teacher read the Bible aloud and talked a while about how Jesus treated all people alike and loved everyone, but Jessie wondered if anyone really got it—even the teacher.

When the class was over, the teacher and all the young ladies dressed in their finery walked out without a word to their guest. Jessie found her way to the sanctuary and joined in the worship service. She sat next to an older lady who looked a little like her grandmother, except she was dressed in what Jessie thought were very expensive clothes and her jewelry and purse looked like something out of a magazine. They sang "How Firm a Foundation" and "I Know Whom I Have Believed," which were familiar hymns to Jessie.

Dr. Cleverdon (she learned that from the worship bulletin) then got up and read Matthew 9:9-13, the same as her Sunday School teacher had. He then talked about how Jesus came "not to call the righteous, but sinners." He was a little more convincing than the Sunday School teacher, but she wasn't sure if he really believed that or not, because she had no interaction with him. When he finished the sermon, the congregation sang "Just As I Am," and then he said the benediction. The lady sitting next to Jessie glanced her way when they stood up, but said nothing.

As they exited the sanctuary through the back doors, Dr. Cleverdon was shaking hands with everyone and talking to some of those who attended, but didn't say anything to Jessie. She realized that most of the ones he talked to had said something about liking his sermon, and he was thanking them. She didn't say anything because she didn't know what to say. The huge limestone columns on the front of the church made her feel small as she made her way down the steps in front of the building.

She caught the next bus back home, and the older man who had been helpful to her in finding her way was already on the bus. "How did you like the church?" he asked.

"It was fine," Jessie said. "But I don't think they liked me much in Sunday School."

"Why do you think that?" he asked.

"Well, when I told them I worked in the shipyards, they acted really weird, like that was an unforgivable sin or something," she told him.

He smiled. "Oh, well, maybe you shouldn't have told them. Some people around here have some strong ideas about people who work down there. But don't you pay any attention to them. You're just as good as they are, no matter how they act."

The man's comments made her feel better, but she still didn't like that class. She thought of her grandmother. *She would be proud of me for going to church, and she would not like the way those people acted.*

The bus was crowded and there was a lot of talking and laughing. There was one young black girl on the back seat. Jessie thought the girl looked like she felt: *alone.* The hymns had been familiar, the sermon had been inspiring, and she decided she did want to go back on Sundays, but not to the Sunday School class.

The next week was Christmas, but the Thompson family paid little attention to it. Chad and Pat invited them over for dinner on Christmas eve, but Bernadette and the girls did no decorating or cooking for the holiday. They only had Christmas Day off, and after Jessie's illness they had little energy for celebrating.

CHAPTER 11

In early spring, baseball was all the rage. When the shipyard team started to play regularly, Jessie and Cornelia went to most of the games when they played at Grayson Stadium. It was reasonably close to Tatnall Homes and easy to find a ride.

"Let's go to the game at Grayson Stadium tomorrow," said Cornelia.

"Who's playing?" asked Jessie.

"Southeastern, of course," replied Cornelia.

"I know that. I mean who are they playing?"

"The Hunter Field Yellow Jackets," said Cornelia.

"Good," said Jessie. "You know that's the team that guy from Mississippi we met the other night plays for—remember?"

"I know," said Cornelia. "Can't wait to see him play."

The next day Cornelia and Jessie, along with several friends who lived in Tatnall, headed out to Grayson Stadium to watch the young men warm up for the game. Donning their jackets and sweaters, they also carried blankets to cover their legs from the late February cold. As it turned out, however, the sun came out by the time the game started and the temperature rose quickly in Savannah. It was a great day for baseball.

"I am glad Jesse Powell's pitching," said Jessie.

"Yeah, you only like him because your name's practically the same," remarked one of her friends.

"No, he's a great pitcher," said Jessie. "You'll see."

"I'm looking for that guy we met at the dance the other night," said Cornelia. "He's cute."

"He doesn't stand a chance against Jesse and Jake Hines though," said Jessie.

"You never know," commented Cornelia. "There's always that chance. But anyway, I'd like to see him. I can't remember his name though."

"I can't either," said Jessie. "But I'll know him if I see him. Oh, there he is! He's playing third base."

"Yes, it is!" exclaimed Cornelia. "What's his number?"

"Twelve," yelled someone. "He's number twelve. I think he's supposed to be good. I think I saw something about him in the *Sou'Easter* when we played them before."

"Well, like I said, I don't think he's better than our guys," added Jessie.

The Yellow Jackets batted first, but when the initial inning was over, Powell had struck out two batters and one guy didn't make it to first base.

By the end of the third inning, there was still no score and Powell had struck out eight of Hunter Field's players. The fans of the shipyard team were getting excited. As Powell kept striking the other team's players out, Jessie looked at her friends and said, "See, I told you!"

In the fifth inning one other Southeastern member hit a single, and Jake Hines scored a run. One of the Yellow Jackets got to first base via a walk, but at the end of the inning the score was still 1-0 in favor of Southeastern's team.

As soon as they began singing "Take Me Out to the Ballgame" during the seventh inning stretch, Jessie noticed the smell of popcorn and began digging in her pocket for the coins she had put there. "Come on," she said to one of the girls. "Let's get some popcorn."

Before they could leave, though, a young boy came strolling down the steps of the stadium shouting, "Peanuts, popcorn, Cracker Jacks!" All the girls turned toward him, getting out their change and trying to decide which treat they wanted. Jessie decided on Cracker Jacks, and Cornelia bought peanuts. They decided to share a soda. Popcorn was the best smell in the world though, as far as Jessie was concerned, so she accepted a handful from one of the other girls.

Powell continued his streak of striking out batters, and no one was scoring. Southeastern fans needed neither coats, sweaters, nor blankets for the cool February weather. They were alive and warm when the game ended with Powell striking out twenty-six batters. Only two of the Yellow Jackets made it to first base. Jake Hines hit three of Southeastern's four singles.

"That is the most exciting game we've had," said Jessie. "Let's go speak to them when they come out."

The girls headed over to the team's dugout. They didn't know all the guys, but they congratulated them cheerfully as the young men came through the gate. Jessie noticed that the guys seemed appreciative, thanking them for attending the game. They all had big smiles on their faces.

Chapter 12

By May of 1944, Jessie had resigned herself to the fact that she would be a year behind her classmates in school. She still hated the idea, but she didn't think about it as often as she had in the fall and she tried to make the best of it. One day Cornelia came home from work excited about the possibility of going to a ship launching the next week. Periodically, she had tried to get Jessie to go, but Jessie always resisted.

"You know I hate all that making a big deal about these ships," said Jessie.

"Yes, I do know. But this launching is different," said Cornelia.

"How?"

"It's being named for one of our favorite people!"

"Who is that?" asked Jessie.

"Juliette Low," answered Cornelia, smiling. "And her niece will be there to christen the ship."

Jessie couldn't believe it! She and Cornelia had read a lot about Juliette Low even before they moved to Savannah because they had both been avid Girl Scouts throughout childhood. Jessie loved being a part of the Scouts because her favorite aunt had been their troop leader. She had never been as good as Cornelia at all their projects, but she enjoyed spending time with her aunt every week. Cornelia handed her the newspaper telling about next week's launching of the *USS Juliette Low*. Jessie read every word before she looked up.

"Okay, I definitely want to go to this one," she said.

A week later, on May 12, Cornelia, Jessie, and Bernadette arrived early enough to check in with their leadermen and obtain clearance to attend the ceremony. Work did not stop for the launchings, but workers were allowed to go as long as they got permission and returned to work as soon as the launching was finished.

Although only a few workers were involved in the actual process of launching the ships, the preparation began about twenty-four hours in advance with the shipwright foreman handing out detailed instructions listing each job to be done and the time to do it. About a dozen shipwrights and burners waited for orders from the shipwright foreman.

As Jessie, Cornelia, and Bernadette crowded in among the excited visitors on the day of the launching of the *USS Juliette Low*, Jessie looked at the sea of faces, including dozens of young Girl Scouts. It reminded her of the many times her aunt had taken her troop to events in celebration of some famous person. But this was a celebration of the Girl Scouts' founder!

They got a place as close to the stage as possible, where they could see and hear everything that went on. The large rectangular area around the platform meant that the crowds had to stand outside the fenced area, so Jessie and her family tried to position themselves far enough back to see the stage, but close enough to hear. The speakers had a microphone, of course, but Jessie and Cornelia wanted to see all those on the stage. Just before the launching, ship officials, visiting dignitaries, and the workers responsible during the ceremony gathered on the platform built high off the ground against the bow of the ship.

The noisy crowd quieted a little, with much whispering and pointing to the different people on the platform. "The woman on the right next to the man must be the niece," said Cornelia. "Her name is Mrs. Samuel Lawrence, from Charleston, West Virginia."

"So, I guess she is the sponsor and will christen the ship," observed Bernadette.

"Yes, and she was the first Girl Scout in the United States," said Jessie.

"Who is the lady on the left?" asked Bernadette.

"She is the president of the Girl Scout Association of Savannah," replied Jessie. "I think her name is Mrs. Johnson, or Johnston, or something. It was in the paper. She is the matron of honor, and would be the one to christen the ship if something happened to the niece."

Jessie couldn't help but wonder why she had never come to a launching before. It was so exciting! The red-white-and-blue bunting draped the bow of the ship, making it look elegant.

On stage it was apparent that the ceremony was about to begin. H. R. Mitchell, head porter in Southeastern's administration building, came on stage with the flowers, ribbons, and the bottle of champagne. At that time the master of ceremonies began introducing those on the stage. He presented Mrs. Lawrence and Mrs. Johnson with the customary flowers. Then he introduced the lady in the middle, Mrs. Bruce McIntosh, who was to give the principal address. Chairman of the Juliette Low Region, she was representing the National Girl Scout Organization. She talked briefly about how the ship would carry goodwill to all the ports of the world, just as Juliette Low had sought to create international friendships.

When Mrs. McIntosh finished her remarks, the announcer introduced Irby Lasseter, a cousin of Juliette Low and a member of one of the troops in Savannah, who presented the ship's flag to Capt. W. F. O'Toole. In presenting the flag, Lasseter commented, "May this flag wave unharmed and symbolize hope for a happier future for the ports of the Seven Seas."

Finally it was time for the actual launch. In the distance Jessie could hear the ship construction still under way—gantries moving, welding torches popping. All the riveting, drilling, and hammering provided a noisy background for the ceremony. But suddenly it became deathly quiet on stage, and the crowd knew the moment for the launching was near.

Jessie knew that timing was critical. Even though she had not attended a launching before, she had heard of all the drama that went along with the launchings. It was considered bad luck if the ship did not get christened properly, so Mrs. Lawrence needed to hear the orders of the shipwright foreman so she could be ready to smash the champagne bottle against the ship at just the right time. Mrs. Lawrence stood ready with the bottle wrapped in red, white, and blue ribbon. The Shipyard Band and the Color Guard (made up of Girl Scouts whose fathers were shipbuilders) had assembled near the stage. Under the bow of the ship there was silence also. Suddenly those near the front heard the foreman's first order: "Get ready! Burn out!"

Mrs. Lawrence appeared a bit nervous, but at just the right time she shouted, "I christen thee *Juliette Low*," and smashed the champagne bottle heavily against the ship. It broke on the first try. Cheers went up from the crowd as the Shipyard Band began playing "Song for the Victory Fleet" and the ship began sliding down the ways toward the water.

For the first time Jessie felt a part of something bigger than just welding a slab of metal. Even though her part may have been small, she began to believe that she had a part in something important. She had been reluctant to buy into the whole patriotic idea that they were helping win the war by working on the home front, but *Juliette Low* almost convinced her.

CHAPTER 13

As spring came along, so again did Jessie's feeling of discontent because she knew that her friends back in Alabama were preparing for high school graduation. When she came home one day and saw a letter from her friend Cassidy, she opened it with both joy and sadness. She always looked forward to any word from home, yet these letters were a reminder of what she was missing. The ones from Cassidy usually recounted the mundane events of her school days, but Jessie loved every word. She ripped open the letter and read hurriedly.

Dear Jessie,

First things first—I got accepted to George Washington University! As you know, I've wanted to go there since middle school. My mom and dad were hoping I would go somewhere closer to home, maybe even in North Carolina, but I am so excited! Maybe you can come too when you get through with making Liberty Ships.

The other thing I wanted to tell you is that I heard some more about Owen and his family. You remember that I told you they had moved to Arizona? Well, I thought they might not get put in the detention camps since they went to Arizona instead of California, but they were put in one in Gila, Arizona. I knew you would want to know. I will write you if I hear any more about them.

Our graduation is May 31. I will be leaving my aunt's here in Alabama the next day and will spend most of the summer with my mom and dad in North Carolina, and then I will head to Washington, D.C.

I hope all is going well for you in Savannah and that you're still meeting lots of handsome soldiers!

Your friend,
Cassidy

Jessie couldn't decide whether she was more upset by learning that Cassidy would be in college in Washington, D.C., by the time she got back to Alabama, or that poor Owen Doi and his family had been put in one of those internment camps. Everything was so crazy lately. Nothing seemed normal in her life—or in anyone else's. She knew she should be happy for Cassidy, but why did she have to go so far away?

After reading Cassidy's letter, Jessie decided she had to do something to calm herself. She knew what she wanted to do. She walked into the kitchen and looked in the cabinet.

"Mom, where is that recipe book you had the other day? I think I'll bake a cake."

"I don't know if we have enough sugar, Jessie."

"That's all right. I can go buy some," said Jessie.

"We may have used all our stamps for this month," responded her mother.

"What do you mean?"

"The government has rationed sugar you know," said Bernadette. "We can only get a certain amount, and I may not have any more stamps to get sugar. I'll look and see."

After looking in the cabinets for sugar and in the drawer where she kept the rationing stamps, Bernadette realized she had no more sugar and no more stamps. "I'm sorry, Jessie," she said.

Jessie pouted. "Can I at least pop some popcorn?"

"Of course," said her mother.

Jessie walked slowly to get the popcorn. "When will this war be over?"

"I don't know, dear. Soon I hope," her mother answered. "What did Cassidy say in her letter today?"

"Nothing much," Jessie said. "Just that she's about to graduate and go off to college. Mama, will I ever really get to go back and finish high school and go to college?"

"Sure you will," said Bernadette.

Jessie popped the corn, and she and her mom ate in silence. "Do you ever hear from my dad?"

"No." It annoyed her that her mother was so reluctant to talk about her dad. Jessie pushed her mother a bit. "Does he have our address?"

"I'm not sure. Your grandmother has it, so he knows how to get it," said her mother. The subject of Dan Thompson always seemed to upset Jessie's mother. She had always seemed bitter after he left.

"I'd like to talk to him about college," she said.

"What good would that do?"

"He might help me pay for it," she said.

"The chances of that are slim," said her mother. "How much has he helped you in the last few years? I can tell you, practically none. He never even sends you a birthday gift. And his Christmas gifts are few."

Jessie tried to remember what her dad looked like. She remembered him playing with her when she was really young, but she couldn't remember much about him. She had only been about five when he left.

After they ate their popcorn, Jessie decided to go to her room and read. She considered writing back to Cassidy, but she could not think of anything interesting to write. Unlike Cassidy, who was planning all sorts of exciting things, Jessie was going to work every day. Who wanted to hear about that?

Cornelia came in as soon as Jessie went to her room, so she decided to talk to her about their dad. She might remember more about what he was really like. "What do you remember about Daddy?" she asked.

"Oh, I remember lots of things. I am a lot like him," Cornelia said.

"What do you mean? How are you like him?"

"Well, he likes all kinds of sports, and he is adventuresome, like I am," she said. "When he comes back, you'll see."

"You think he'll really come back?"

"Of course," said Cornelia. "He told me that one day he'd be back. He said he just had to go out and see the world."

"Well, I don't really believe he'll be back, but I wish he'd at least help me with college," said Jessie.

On the evening of June 6 the main news was that the Allied forces had invaded France at Normandy Beach. The excitement in the voices of the reporters confirmed that this was a major accomplishment, and even though Jessie knew little of what really happened, she looked at the map of France and got a general idea of the significance of the news. After that, there was some talk of the "winding down of the war in Europe," which was encouraging to her.

CHAPTER 14

The next day Jessie was surprised when she came home to find a letter from Al Donaldson. She went straight to her room and sat down on her bed. She had not heard much from him since his leave, and she had decided that he might not ever come back to Savannah. But here was a letter! She tore it open and smoothed out the creases so she could read it.

Dear Jestina,

I hope this finds you well. I am fine. I've been really busy lately, but I wanted to let you know that I have a few days off at the end of the month and will be at the base in Savannah. I hope I can see you while I'm there. I am still not sure which day I'll arrive, but it's sometime the last week of the month. I'll find a way to get you word when I get there.

Your friend with no hair,
Al

Jessie laughed out loud at this closing, and suddenly the world seemed brighter, just thinking of Al. About that time Cornelia walked in the room.

"You look happy," she said.

Jessie waved the letter. "Remember my friend Al? He's going to be in Savannah a few days near the end of the month.

"That guy with no hair? You really like him, don't you?"

"Actually I do," said Jessie. "He is a really nice fellow."

"Well, great. I'm glad he's coming then," said Cornelia.

The month flew by and it was the week Al was supposed to be there. Jessie started anticipating his arrival on Monday, but she heard nothing—on Monday, or on Tuesday, or on Wednesday. *What if he didn't come? What if he decided not to contact her?*

On Thursday she was determined not to even think he was coming. She stood around and talked to friends after work, and then walked home extra slowly. She refused to even look down the street as she approached her house. She moped along, looking down at her feet. When she got right in front of her house, she heard someone speak her name. She looked up to see Al sitting on her porch steps.

"Where have you been? Cornelia and your mother have been here for half an hour."

"Oh, I was just talking with some friends," she said. "I had no idea you'd be here today."

"This is the last week of the month you know, and it's Thursday, almost the last day of the week," he said, grinning at her.

"Well, I'm glad you made it," she said, sitting down beside him on the porch step.

"I'm sorry I didn't call you before I came. It was too late when I got to the base last night, and I knew you'd be at work all day today."

"I know. How have you been?"

"It's been crazy. It's a crazy world now. I never thought I'd be in the middle of a war, but now it seems everyone is—even the women!"

"Yes. Everywhere you look around the shipyard, and even in the city of Savannah, there are signs encouraging people to join in the 'war effort,' and many of them are especially directed at women," said Jessie.

They sat and talked for a while, until it was getting dark. Jessie finally asked, "Do you want to go inside?"

"I'd better head on back to the base. I wanted to see if you could go out tomorrow night after work. I really miss the times we went down to that Johnny Harris restaurant on Victory Drive and ate and then danced for a while. They had the best fried chicken I'd ever eaten."

"I'm sure I can. I'll have to ask Mom, but I'm sure she'll let me."

"Do you think Cornelia would like to get a friend and go with us?"

"Let's ask her before you leave, so you'll know."

Jessie stood up and went to the door. "Cornelia!" she yelled.

"Coming," Jessie heard her sister say. In a few seconds, Cornelia was at the door.

"Al and I are going to Johnny Harris tomorrow night. Want to invite a friend and come along?"

"Well, yes, but did you ask Mom?"

"Not yet," Jessie said, stepping into the living room and calling to her mom. When Bernadette came into the room and Jessie asked her if it was okay, her mom said it was.

"What time can you girls be ready?" asked Al. "One of my friends has a car, and he said I could borrow it tomorrow night because he's working."

Cornelia looked at Jessie. "Six?" she asked.

"Sounds fine to me," answered Jessie.

Getting out of bed was easy the next morning, because for Jessie every hour of the day brought her one hour closer to the end of the day and her plans for Friday evening. On their way home that evening, she and Cornelia discussed what they'd wear.

"What are you wearing?" asked Cornelia. "Can I wear your red sweater with my new black skirt?"

"I guess," said Jessie. "I'm trying to decide. I like that light blue blouse I bought, but I don't have anything to wear with it. I may see what that lavender dress with the circular skirt looks like on me. I keep changing my mind."

"I called Edward and asked him to go with me," said Cornelia. "I know he likes red, and he's a really good dancer."

"Al is a good dancer too," said Jessie. "But I really don't know what colors he likes."

"I think Al likes whatever color you have on," laughed Cornelia.

Jessie blushed. She thought it was probably true. Al always complimented her, no matter what she wore. As soon as the girls got home, they started getting ready to go. Each of them tried on several outfits, but in the end Cornelia wore the red sweater and black skirt, and Jessie wore the lavender dress. Jessie felt proud as they got in the car with Al.

When they walked into the Johnny Harris ballroom, it was crowded and looked even more beautiful than Jessie remembered. She looked around at all the ladies in their party dresses. Although her dress was not as fancy as some, it blended in well. The lights from the ceiling looked like twinkling stars. She smiled at Al as they were led to one of the tall polished wood booths.

"I know what you will order," Jessie said to Al as he opened his menu.

Al laughed. "But I have no idea what you'll order," he said.

"Actually, I want the fried chicken too," she said.

"Good. We think alike."

After they ordered, all four of them joined several others on the dance floor and danced until they saw their food coming out.

Only once that evening did Jessie notice some people staring at Al's bald head, and she felt that Cornelia and Edward accepted him as he was, which was easy to do with Al. He was such an honest and sincere person, and he was interesting too. He had an intense and important job, and it wasn't long before he had captured all of their attention as they listened to his stories. After they finished dinner, they danced again for a while until they realized it was time to go home.

When Al and Edward dropped the girls off, Al told Jessie he would be leaving on Monday, but could come over and visit for a while on Sunday if that would be okay. Of course it was.

Later that evening as she and Cornelia were getting ready for bed, Jessie said, "That was the best time I've had since we've been in Savannah. I didn't think of home even once tonight."

"I had a good time too, little sister," said Cornelia. "Al really is a nice fellow. Do you think you'll keep up with him, even after the war is over?"

"I don't know. Maybe. Everything just seems so uncertain. I'm afraid to think whether Al will even live to the end of the war. He's doing such a dangerous job. You know the stress is what caused him to lose his hair."

"Yes, I heard him say that. Well, I hope he will be safe."

"Me too. He says he wants to continue his education after he gets out of the service—just like I do," said Jessie.

Sunday afternoon came and Jessie dreaded saying goodbye to Al, but looked forward to having some time to visit. She made some lemonade and cookies and brought them out to the porch so they could talk.

"Are you going on more bombing missions?" Jessie asked.

"I never know, but probably."

"Tell me about the B-17 bomber. I've heard it's really important—and a dangerous mission."

Al looked out over the lawn. "Yeah, it's pretty special. It's called 'Flying Fortress' and was designed in 1935. The reason they say it is so dangerous is because we have to fly during the day for better visibility, but lack of cover means that we have more losses also."

Jessie shook her head. "I'm glad I don't have to do that. I'd be scared to death!"

"It all gets routine when you're out there," he said. "But of course, it is dangerous. War is dangerous."

"I admire you for being willing to do it, but I worry about you, knowing what you're doing out there. When will you have another leave?"

"First, I guess I need to tell you that it may be a while before I'll be back in Georgia. I'll be going back to Oklahoma when I'm on leave at Christmas.

My folks have been really upset that I never manage to get home, so I have a few extra days off then and can go see them."

"I don't blame you. Are all three of your sisters still at home?"

"Two of them are and the oldest one is now in college, and she'll be home at Christmas. I'm impressed that you remembered that I have three sisters!"

"I keep up with things like that," she laughed. "What are your sisters like? Are they like you?"

"Well, the two older ones are very 'girlie' I guess, but I think I made my baby sister a tomboy. After my dad died, I had to take care of her a lot, and I taught her to play ball and do all sorts of boy games, so she's always been a very outdoor, boyish kind of sister."

"I bet you and your family have a lot of fun together," Jessie said.

"Yes, we do, and I miss them a lot. Fortunately, they all write me letters regularly."

"I guess you look forward to those letters."

"Oh I sure do! We all compete over who gets the most letters. You could write me too, you know. That'd increase my chances of being the winner!"

"Okay. I'll do it." Jessie got a piece of notebook paper and had him write down his address.

"Just remember that everything is monitored now, and when we get your letter it's photocopied and put on some sort of newsreel and then recopied when it gets overseas. Don't say anything that would give the Germans any information, or they'll black it out."

"Really? I don't even know what that would be," said Jessie.

"Well, I don't either really, but this guy on my crew, his dad sent him a letter and a lot of it was blacked out, so just keep it simple. Just don't say anything about where you work or what you're doing. I'm sure they wouldn't want you saying anything about building Liberty Ships for the war effort!" Al stood up, signaling that it was time to go. "I'll write you when I get back to my station."

"Do you think the war will be over soon, since the Normandy invasion?" asked Jessie.

"I really don't know. I know that's what they want people to think, but I just don't know."

He and Jessie said their goodbyes and promised to write one another. As he left, Jessie realized he was probably as good a friend as she'd ever had.

CHAPTER 15

After Al returned to his mission, he and Jessie wrote almost every week. She wished he could write about his work. He usually referred to the group of men as "the boys and I" in his letters. He never actually said where he was, but he would sometimes say things such as "looking out our back window, I see a herd of sheep," or he would comment on the size of his bed or mention being crowded. Nothing he said could have helped the enemy determine where he was located.

To learn more about Al's job, Jessie decided she would read about the B-17 bombers described in newspapers and magazines. The B-17 had been around in some form since 1935, but the current model had been redesigned a few times. She read about several of the responsibilities of the crew members, and she knew that Al was the bombardier. Now she would not have to rely on his letters to have a better understanding of what he was doing. Nevertheless, she always looked forward to his letters. They were always amusing, and she could imagine what he was doing, but she also remembered him saying, "Just remember that the people on the news only tell things that make all this war stuff sound great, but believe me, it's not." One evening after a stressful day at the shipyards, she was especially excited to see a letter from him.

Dear Jestina,

I hope you are well. It is nine o'clock Sunday morning here, and the morning's fog has already lifted. We have a day off, and the boys and I (except for Charlie) are going to a chapel for church. Billy talked in his sleep off and on all night last night, so none of us got much sleep.

This little town is older than any I have ever seen in the States. There are some kind of red flowers growing outside our window, and you can see the beautiful forest on a nearby mountain. I don't know how long we will be here, but we are enjoying the gorgeous scenery while we are here. Since it's been dry, I'm thinking you may be seeing signs of fall in Georgia, but it's still lush and green here. They say it gets cold here in the winter, but the weather is just about right at this time of year. Who knows where we'll be by winter anyway? One of our crew members says he will be transferring to another division next month, but I haven't heard anything about a change.

I hope you are still enjoying work and going to movies and dances. Tell Cornelia and your mother hello for me and keep those letters coming!

Sincerely,
Al

Jessie always looked forward to Al's letters, but she was always disappointed too. She felt like he was just making up things to say that really didn't tell anything about what he was doing. Sometimes she hated that! She wanted to know where he was, what he was doing, when he was dropping bombs, anything but all this describing the landscape and telling virtually nothing. But if he had told anything, they would have probably blacked it out.

Although Jessie had never been that interested in the news, she now listened to the evening broadcast. That evening in August, she made it a point to pay attention to the news on the radio and to read the newspaper. When the reporters announced that Paris had been liberated from the Nazis, she felt it more than likely that Al had been in a Flying Fortress during the liberation. Al always said that the term "Fortress" was probably an exaggeration. Otherwise, why did they need the four gunners on the crew for defense?

CHAPTER 16

By the fall of 1944, Jessie had resigned herself to the fact that, as much as she hated it, she would be missing another year of school. Although she wasn't imagining her friends and their experiences as she had last fall, she still thought about the fact that she was missing out on her final year of school. As much as she resented being unable to go back home, she also had become accustomed to her life in Savannah.

She and Cornelia enjoyed meeting many soldiers from the base and going to movies and dances with the other young people, and she even enjoyed the comradeship with the other shipyard employees—sometimes. Another positive was that she and Cornelia were getting along really well. Back in Alabama, since Cornelia was older and they each had their own set of friends and different interests, Cornelia had tended to ignore Jessie. In Savannah, she often treated her as an equal.

The day began as any other Monday that fall. During the weekend, she and Cornelia had gone to see a movie with some friends on Friday night, and a dance at Johnny Harris on Saturday night. Jessie had gone to church on Sunday morning and read a chapter in *Little Women* that afternoon while Cornelia and Bernadette went for a walk. Then they all three took a nap before the evening meal.

On Monday morning they all checked in at the gate and then waved goodbye hurriedly so they would not be late arriving at their respective work sites.

The September sun was still hot in Savannah, and Jessie wiped sweat from her face with her sleeve. Her mother always insisted that she wear long sleeves to protect her skin from sunburn. She knew it was close to lunch time because she saw several other welders stop at the end of a run and start putting up their equipment, but Jessie was carefully finishing out her last seam. As soon as she stopped, she noticed that her supervisor was standing there watching.

She looked up at him and noticed that he had a peculiar look on his face. "Jessie?" he said, as if confirming who she was.

"Yes," she answered.

"Come with me," he said. She wanted to say "Why?" as she followed him down toward the administration building, but somehow she knew she didn't really want to know.

The short trip seemed to take hours, and Jessie's heart was racing when they entered the building and headed for her supervisor's office. "Have a seat and wait here," he said, turning around and stepping outside the door. Then she heard her mother's voice and the supervisor saying, "Come on in."

As soon as she saw her mother's face, she knew something was terribly wrong. Tears were streaming down Bernadette's face. "It's—it's Cornelia, honey," she said. "There's been a terrible accident."

"Where is she?" asked Jessie. "Can I see her?"

"No, not right now," said her supervisor. "She's in the infirmary. But Mrs. Thompson, it's not good. She's—she's gone, I'm afraid."

"But what happened to her?" shouted Jessie.

"We haven't got the whole story, Miss Thompson, but she fell from the top of the ship somehow. We'll know more details when the workers are asked about the exact circumstances. The supervisor and some of her coworkers are still at the infirmary."

Jessie looked at her mother, and then they reached out and put their arms around each other and stood in the office until the gentlemen took them down to another office to wait for a report. They sat in silence for what seemed like an eternity before a few men came in and started talking to Bernadette. Jessie kept hearing things like "We are so sorry" and "I am the president of the company" (she thought). As far as Jessie was concerned, they were just all trying to excuse themselves for letting her sister get hurt. As she listened to them saying that very few people had been hurt at the shipyard, that they tried to make the workplace safe, she became more and more angry.

Suddenly she was shouting, "I don't care if not many people have got hurt! I care about my sister getting hurt! Stop making excuses! Just stop!" She put her hands over her ears, and began to sob.

"I hate you! I hate this place! I hate your excuses! You don't care about me or my family. All you care about are these stupid ships and getting them done fast, even if people get hurt!" Her mother tried to calm her as they led her down the hall toward the outside. Moving as if in a fog, Jessie was taken home finally. She couldn't remember how she got there, but she was in her living room with some of her coworkers and some of her neighbors.

All evening, neighbors dropped by with food. Their cousin Chad and his family came over and helped Bernadette make arrangements for Cornelia's body to be taken back to Alabama. Some other Southeastern executives came over and offered help taking the family back for the service.

"I think we've got everything worked out now for getting you and Jessie to Alabama and back," said Chad. "You'll need to call the pastor at your church and work with him and the funeral home there to arrange for the service."

"Thank you," said Bernadette through tears. "I appreciate your help. I just couldn't do it by myself."

All Jessie could think about was how she had warned Cornelia that it was dangerous up on the ways, and she had even told her mother that they could get killed. Now maybe her mother would listen. But at least now they were going home.

"What should I take with me? Are we just going for the week and then coming back for our things, or what?" she asked her mother.

"No, we'll be coming back after the funeral. The supervisors said we could take off the rest of the week."

"You mean you intend to come back and work here again?" she asked.

"Of course, Jessie. We have to," said her mother.

"Why?"

"We have jobs here. We can't just quit."

"I can. I hate it here. I can go back to work at the five and dime store where I worked before we came. And you can go back to the telephone company."

"But we're making twice or three times here what we can make back home. We just can't quit our jobs here. Besides, we are really needed here to help build the ships. Our men in the service are depending on us."

Jessie sighed heavily. She couldn't believe her mother would actually decide to stay on at a place where her daughter was killed doing her work. She turned around and went into her room and burst into tears.

They left Wednesday morning on the train bound for Atlanta. Jessie's aunt and uncle would meet them in Atlanta and take them back to Alabama. The trip was long, but Jessie slept most of the way. She saw her aunt and uncle as soon as they got off the train, and her uncle told the ladies to wait while he retrieved their luggage. It was good to see her relatives, and the ride back to Alabama was reassuring. She couldn't wait to see her grandmother and Aunt Lexie. She was hoping one of them might convince her mother to stay, but inside she knew it would not happen.

At times she was seething inside with anger at her mother, at everyone. Of course she knew her mother was grieving too, but in Jessie's mind the right thing to do was to quit working at that place where they let Cornelia get killed. Someone should have been assigned to have kept her from falling from the top of the ship. In the back of her mind she knew that Cornelia would not have wanted someone watching after her. But it didn't matter. She got hurt and Jessie was furious with everyone who might have kept her safe, but didn't.

It was an emotional meeting with Jessie's grandmother when they arrived, and again the next morning when they went to see Aunt Lexie. By noon, Bernadette was exhausted and decided to go home and take a nap.

Jessie wanted to go see Mr. and Mrs. Cohen, Cassidy's uncle and aunt, to learn whether she was happy at George Washington University and what they had heard from her. Mrs. Cohen hugged Jessie.

"I heard about Cornelia. I am so, so sorry," she said. "When is the service?"

"It's Friday at two, at the church," replied Jessie.

"How long will you be in town?" she asked.

"I think we have to go back Sunday, but I'm not sure." Jessie wanted to say that she didn't want to go back at all, but decided against it.

"You haven't heard from Cassidy, have you?" asked Mrs. Cohen.

"No. Have you?"

"As a matter of fact, she called us last week. You know she went to Washington, D.C., to attend George Washington University?" Jessie nodded. "We assumed she would be taking classes by now. But when she called she said she was going to be working for the government."

"Oh my goodness!" said Jessie. "What will she be doing?"

"She didn't seem to know. The only thing she said about it is that they told her the university had given them her name and that she was qualified to do what they needed."

"Will she work there in D.C.?" asked Jessie.

"She said she didn't know."

"Do you think she'll call again?"

"No. She said she would not be able to call once she started work. She said she could write letters, but that they would all be read by her supervisors and anything with any mention of where she was or what she was doing would be blacked out," said Mrs. Cohen.

"Wow! That sounds exciting! I sure wish I could talk to her," said Jessie.

"Yes, I wish I could too. I hope she is not in any danger," said Mrs. Cohen. "She is like a daughter to me now."

Before Jessie left, she gave Mrs. Cohen her address and asked her to write her if she learned anything new from Cassidy

When Jessie left Mrs. Cohen's house, she decided to drop by and speak to Aunt Lexie again for a few minutes, since she lived just a few houses down. As soon as she went in, she confronted her aunt with the fact that she wanted to move back to Alabama. Aunt Lexie listened carefully to all Jessie said, including the fact that Cornelia had chosen to work in a riskier place than Jessie and Bernadette had.

"Do you fear getting hurt in the work you do?" she asked.

"No."

"What about your mother? Is her work unsafe?"

"I don't think so," said Jessie. "But I don't like it there."

"You might want to compare the money you make there with what you can make here. Also, remember that Cornelia liked what she did. She chose to do it, knowing that there was danger. I think I know how you feel, but be honest about why you want to come back. You have always resented going there and missing your last year of school. But none of that will change if you come back now. And nothing can bring Cornelia back."

"But don't you want me to come home?"

"Of course I'd love having you here. But I can't honestly think of a reason to convince Bernadette to come back if she doesn't want to. It wouldn't really solve any of her problems—or yours, for that matter."

Jessie left feeling somewhat betrayed by her aunt. She had always felt that her Aunt Lexie was on her side about things. Of course, she knew that her aunt was right in what she said. Still, she wanted someone on her side.

That night Jessie thought back over her visit with Mrs. Cohen. *Cassidy is working for the government! Oh, if only I could talk to my friend. Maybe one day I can! If Cassidy is a part of winning the war, maybe I should think about doing my part too—but I don't want to.*

The small church in the middle of town was filled when the Thompsons arrived. A hush came over the crowd as they walked in with the organ playing "Rock of Ages" and Jessie stepped a bit closer to her mother. Her first thought was that the energetic Cornelia would hate this. The pastor gave a few words of comfort, and then talked about how he remembered Cornelia as a child and teenager being so enthusiastic about all her endeavors. What he did not say was that she never attended church during her teen years. A soloist sang "When the Morning Comes," and then the service was over and the coffin was rolled out of the church. Everyone followed it up the hill to the cemetery.

Jessie could hardly breathe. She thought she would smother before they got to the top of the hill. Noticing that her mother looked as if she might collapse, she grabbed her left arm just as her uncle took hold of her right one. Her mother did not collapse, but she seemed very weak.

When they got to the grave site, the pastor read a psalm, said a prayer, and gave her and her mother and grandmother a flower. When they stood up and Jessie realized they were about to lower Cornelia's body into the hole they had dug, she pulled away from her mother and started running back down the hill. She knew she was abandoning her mother at a bad time, but she could not stand it any longer.

She heard someone calling her name, and then she heard footsteps behind her, but she kept running until she got back to the steps of the church. She sat down and put her head in her hands. She felt a man's hand on her shoulder, and a slightly familiar voice called her name. She looked up. It was her father sitting beside her. She had not realized he was there, because he had arrived late and sat in the back of the church during the service.

It took her a few seconds to take it all in. She had not even thought about the possibility of him being there. It made sense that her grandmother or mother would have contacted him, but it had just not occurred to her. A mixture of gratitude and anger flowed through her. She stared at this man she barely knew. Who was he?

"Why are you here? It's too late now!" she sobbed, remembering Cornelia's words about how he would be back. "She doesn't need you now! None of us do. Just go on back to seeing the world, or whatever it is you've been doing!"

He kept his hand on her shoulder and did not respond immediately. Finally, he said. "You're right. I'm too late. No one knows that more than I do." They sat there in silence until the little group came back down the hill from the cemetery. When they got close, her father got up and walked to meet her mother and grandmother, then spoke briefly to them and left.

When they returned to her grandmother's house, neighbors and friends had brought all kinds of food as they always did after a funeral, but Jessie could not eat anything. Her anger was boiling up in her stomach—at her father, her mother, the shipyard company, God, and even Cornelia, for wanting to work in a dangerous situation instead of a safe one. The only person she did not hold anger against was her grandmother.

Her grandmother put her arms around her and gave her some comfort. Jessie just wanted to stay with her and receive the unconditional love her grandmother always gave her. But that night when she told her grandmother she did not want to go back to Savannah, her grandmother asked her a question that challenged her to really think about her situation.

"What do you think Cornelia would want you to do?"

"I don't know." But of course she did. Cornelia would want her to go back and finish the job they'd started. The adventurous Cornelia would want her little sister to continue to challenge the wrongs of the world by staying the course at the shipyards and then going on to college as she had planned.

On Sunday morning Jessie's aunt and uncle arrived at her grandmother's house early to transport her and her mother back to the train station in Atlanta. Jessie's thoughts turned to the reality that faced them without Cornelia. Amid the anger she felt at so many others, she began to sort out her own mistakes.

She was sorry she could not remember exactly what her last conversation had been with her sister. She was sorry she did not tell her dad that Cornelia bragged about being a lot like him. She was sorry she'd told him she didn't need him, because she knew she did. By the time they reached Atlanta, she had decided to work on doing the right thing, because the one thing she'd learned for sure was that you don't always know what the day will bring to your life.

"Thank you so much for bringing us back to Atlanta," she said as she hugged her aunt and uncle. Her uncle got their luggage and headed into the station while she and her mother followed along with her aunt.

"We were glad to do what we could," said her aunt. "Please keep in touch. Call us when you get to Savannah."

"We will," said Bernadette. Jessie could see the weight of the world on her mother's face. There were more wrinkles than before, and her eyes looked a bit red and swollen. She had said little since the funeral, and Jessie wondered whether her mother blamed herself for Cornelia's death. She had to admit that one of her first thoughts was that her mother should have told Cornelia not to volunteer to work up on the ways. But now she was not so sure. Cornelia would probably have insisted on it anyway.

When they boarded the train, they were already tired from getting up so early, so they both soon nodded off to sleep. When Jessie awoke a while later, her mother was already awake and handed her the small package her grandmother had given them as they left. It contained some popcorn, along with a candy bar and an apple for each of them. They munched on the popcorn for a bit, and then Jessie asked her mother about something that had been bugging her since the funeral.

"What did Daddy do after the funeral? Did you talk to him?"

"He said he had to leave. I was not sure he would come at all," she said. "Lexie called him. She keeps in touch I think. I would not have even known how to contact him."

Jessie didn't know whether she should press forward with the conversation, knowing that her mother was grief-stricken, but she needed to learn a little about what had happened to make her mother so bitter toward her father. "So what happened to you and Daddy? Did he just leave? Did you have a fight? Did he leave with someone else?"

Her mother looked at her. "He didn't leave with anyone. He just said he needed to travel, and that he'd decided he didn't want to be tied down with a wife and kids. Something like that."

"So, basically he didn't want to take care of Cornelia and me."

"No. I don't think it was that. In fact, he really seemed to enjoy you kids. That's what I found so strange. He was good with you and Cornelia. And he was always so proud of both of you. He was more patient than I was. But he just left, and that's all there is to it." Jessie could tell that her mother did not intend to say more. It was more than she'd ever said before. Jessie just had to have the answer to one more question.

"Mom, do you have his address? I would like to write him a letter."

"No, I don't. But your Aunt Lexie does, and you could call her and get it I guess."

"Okay. I will." Jessie looked at her mother, noting the weariness in her eyes. "You don't mind if I do that, do you?"

"No, of course not," said her mother.

As the train neared Savannah, Jessie began to imagine going back in the house and into her room and Cornelia not being there—ever again. She didn't think she could sleep there now. Chad met them at the train station and took them to his home, where they had dinner and visited for a while. When it was time to go home, Chad drove them home and unloaded their luggage. Unlike the way she had imagined it, being near Cornelia's belongings brought a sense of familiarity to Jessie, and since she was exhausted, she fell asleep immediately and did not awaken until the morning.

CHAPTER 17

The first few seconds of hearing the alarm at her bedside seemed familiar and routine until Jessie opened her eyes, looked around the room, and saw Cornelia's bed. Then reality struck as she shut off the alarm. Cornelia would never be there again.

Steeling herself against the truth, Jessie climbed out of bed and faced the day. Get up. Get dressed and go to work—without her sister. Her stomach churned. She dreaded the day. She dreaded talking to her mother, but she knew her mother was experiencing even more pain.

She went through the familiar motions. She heard her mother in the kitchen, making breakfast as she always did, except not for Cornelia. Despite her anger and frustration, Jessie did feel compassion for her mother. By the time Jessie got to the kitchen, her mother had a bit of breakfast ready, and they sat down to eat before heading to work.

Checking in at the gate, her mother (for the first time) turned and gave her a quick hug before heading to her own work site. When Jessie got to Number 6 Slab, Sam was there waiting for her.

"Jessie, I am so very sorry about your sister," she said, giving her a hug.

"Thank you," said Jessie. She started to say something else, but choked up and headed on over to pick up her equipment.

"I've missed you," Sam said, when Jessie returned with her welding gear. She left it at that, and Jessie was glad.

At lunch the two talked about the usual work-related things, avoiding the subject on both their minds. Finally Sam said, "I know it's hard for you to talk about—and you don't have to—but I just want you to know that if there's anything I can do to make things easier here at work, please tell me."

"Thank you. I will. It'll just take time I guess," said Jessie.

"Can I ask you one question?" Sam said.

"Of course."

"Do you think there is anything that could have been done to prevent her falling?"

"I don't really know," said Jessie. "I wish I could blame someone, but honestly I don't know. I guess I'm just walking in a fog right now, not knowing what to think or do."

"I understand," said Sam. "I think I felt that way when Mama died. I was only ten. She had been sick for a long time, and I guess I knew she was dying, but didn't really want to admit it. For several weeks after she died I kept going back and forth between being very angry and then trying to do what I thought my mother would want me to do."

"I think I'm just mostly staying angry," said Jessie. "But I do feel sorry for my mother."

"I was very angry at my dad. I'm not sure why. I guess he was angry too. But we didn't talk much. My older brother was fifteen, and he tried to console me, but nothing much helped."

"I've been very angry with my dad too. He left us when I was very young—about six I think. My mom never talked about him much, and I think she's still bitter about the whole thing. He came to the funeral, and it made me so mad."

"Why? Wasn't that a good thing?" asked Sam.

"I guess, but it made me mad because Cornelia always wanted him to come back, and she thought he would. But he didn't—until it was too late—so it made me so angry. I yelled at him."

"What did he do?"

"He sat there for a bit, and then he left. Now I feel sort of bad about the whole thing. But what I said was true. I guess I just don't know the whole story."

"I think your dad probably understands that you are very hurt right now. He'll probably come back around sometime."

"Maybe. I hope so. Do you believe in God?" asked Jessie.

"Yes, I do," affirmed Sam.

"People always say God is like a father, but I hardly know my father. And if God is like that, he doesn't do much for me."

"When I lost my mother I didn't know much about God. My mother had always gone to church, and she had a friend who has helped me a lot. There's still much I don't understand, but I do find comfort in reading the Bible, and I go to church regularly now."

"I used to go to church with my grandmother when we lived in Alabama, but I've only been once or twice here, and I didn't enjoy it much. Maybe I should give it another try."

After checking the time, Jessie and Sam gathered up the remnants of their lunches and headed back to work.

After that, Jessie and Sam always had lunch together and often talked about Jessie's grief over losing her sister. Throughout the fall and into the winter months, Jessie's grief was severe, but talking to Samantha always helped. One day as the two were sitting down to eat their lunches, two girls walked by them and kept staring.

Jessie stared back. "What?" she said. The girls just laughed, but said nothing.

Sam said, "You know why they were staring."

"It's none of their business," said Jessie. Sam seemed to take the discrimination in stride, but the more she saw of it, the more unfair it seemed to Jessie.

As the reality of Cornelia's death settled in on Jessie's life, she became less interested in going out to the movies and dances they had enjoyed so much. The only girl she could imagine going with to those events was Samantha, and she knew that could not happen, so most nights she stayed home. If Al had been there, she might have gone, but of course he wasn't. She wondered if he was still flying on those bombers, or if he had already been killed. She had no way of knowing.

CHAPTER 18

As the flowers lost their bright colors and much of the foliage turned from green to brown that fall, Jessie's mood continued to mimic the sadness of nature. Most weeks Jessie and her mother worked six days, but occasionally they had a Saturday off. Those weekends seemed especially long to her. Part of the weekend was taken up with doing laundry and cleaning house, but still Saturdays were usually boring for Jessie.

At breakfast one Saturday morning Bernadette said, "Why don't we take the bus downtown today and see if we can find you a couple of new sweaters for the winter?"

"If you want to," Jessie said, remembering a similar Saturday last fall when Cornelia had been so excited about shopping for a red sweater.

"If we hurry, we can catch the bus that comes around ten o'clock and be there before noon. We could have lunch downtown too." Jessie knew that her mother was trying to cheer her up, and decided to go along with her efforts.

"Okay," she said. "Oh, I brought the rationing stamp that Chad gave me to buy a pair of shoes. Can I get them today?"

"Yes, I had forgotten about that, but if you can find some, we'll get them."

"Could we look for a place that sells books too? I would really like to find a book or two."

"All right," said her mother. "We can look. I don't remember seeing a place that sells books, but I know there is a news stand near one of the department stores, so we might find some place where you could buy a book. Do you have any particular book in mind?"

"No, I just want to look."

"Well, we'll do that." Jessie's mother was really trying to help her through this troubling time, and she was grateful for it.

They just barely arrived at the bus stop by ten o'clock. When they boarded the bus, Jessie was trying to estimate how long it would take to get to one of the department stores.

"Where are the clothing stores?" she asked.

"I think we'll go down to the area where Adler's is located. It's on Broughton, maybe about at the corner of Broughton and Bull Street. I think there may be some other places within walking distance from there. Anyway, we'll just head there first."

The sun was bright on the colorful leaves of fall that Saturday morning, and it was not long before they were downtown. When they got off the bus, Jessie stretched out her arms and soaked in the sun and the cool, crisp air. "It feels good out here, doesn't it?" she said to her mother. Bernadette nodded.

"I think Adler's is down this way," she said. "But if you see a bookshop or newsstand along the way, we can stop wherever you want to."

They turned the corner and saw the store. "There it is!" shouted Jessie.

Bernadette led the way through the store as they looked at clothes, jewelry, shoes, and purses, picking up various items and inspecting them along the way. "Did you see anything you'd like to go back and look at now, or do you want to go to the shoe store?"

"Let's go to the shoe store!" Jessie hated having only those flimsy cardboard shoes that had practically fallen apart in the last rain. She hadn't realized until then how hard it was to get shoes these days, but her mother had explained to her that because of the war, they had rationed the amount of leather you could buy. That was when Chad had said she could use the stamp they had to buy her some shoes.

The shoe store was close by, and Jessie knew she wanted some black patent leather shoes she had seen in the window a week or so ago. As soon as they walked in, she saw them on the display shelf and showed them to her mother. She got out her rationing stamp, showed it to the clerk, and asked how much the shoes cost.

When the clerk answered, Jessie almost panicked, but her mother said it was okay and paid for them. The cost of leather was outrageous.

As soon as they were outside, Jessie asked, "Does Kress have a lunch counter?"

"I'm not sure, but I was planning to go to Morrison's for lunch. Did you want to run into Kress's anyway?"

"Let's just go in and see if they might have some books," said Jessie. They went in and looked around. Jessie saw a necklace she liked and held it up to her and looked into a mirror nearby. She decided it was too long. She did not see any books, and by that time she was hungry.

"Okay, let's go to Morrison's," she said.

Just as they sat down at Morrison's, Bernadette asked, "Where are your shoes?" Jessie looked down at the seat when she realized the truth. She must have laid them down when she picked up the necklace at Kress's.

"I left them in Kress's! I'll be right back." She ran all the way back to the store.

When she entered the store, she went straight to the counter where she had looked at the necklace. It was lying right where she had put it after trying it on, but she looked all around and did not see the package with her shoes in it. She saw a clerk she had seen when they were in the store before, and walked over to her.

"Did you find a package lying over by the jewelry counter?" she asked. "I left some shoes I bought in here."

"I haven't seen a package like that," replied the clerk. Jessie was sure she was lying.

"Are you sure? Would someone else have seen it?" she asked, her heart sinking.

"No. I am the only clerk in this part of the store. You must have left them somewhere else."

"No, I didn't. I haven't been anywhere else. They have to be here," Jessie insisted.

Jessie was sure the woman was not telling her the truth, and she was almost in tears. Just as she was about to leave, another lady came over. "What's the problem?" she asked.

"Did you see a bag with some shoes in it? This girl thinks she left one here," said the clerk.

"As a matter of fact, I did," said the lady. "It's right over here under the counter."

Jessie's face brightened. "Oh, thank you, thank you!" she said. "I was about to panic. I knew it had to be here, because this was the only place I'd been after I bought the shoes."

She left the store and practically danced all the way back to Morrison's.

After lunch Jessie and Bernadette walked down to Sears and looked around, where Bernadette found a lightweight jacket and Jessie found a sweater. They decided to go back to Adler's where they had both seen some sweaters they liked. Jessie had bought a navy-colored one at Sears.

"What do you think about this rose-colored sweater?" she asked her mother, holding it up for Bernadette to see.

"I like it," said her mother. "I think I'll get this green one."

They were soon finished. When they paid for the sweaters, Bernadette said, "Okay. I think we're finished except for your books. Let's look around a bit and see if we can find some place that sells books."

A few blocks down, Jessie pointed down a side street. "Doesn't that say 'Books and Magazines'?"

"I believe you are right," said her mother.

The small bookstore was just what Jessie had hoped for. It had a good selection of books, so she decided on two she had been wanting to read: *Heidi* and *Tess of the D'Urbervilles*, a book Cassidy had told her about a long time ago. Her mother let her buy both of them. She couldn't wait to begin reading them.

"Wow! This has been a long day," exclaimed Jessie when they got back on the bus. "Thank you for taking me shopping."

"You are welcome," said her mother. "I know these last few weeks have been especially difficult for you. I wanted you to enjoy something."

"Mama," Jessie said, "What do you think about God? Do you have faith in God?"

"I used to," said her mother. "Now I'm not so sure."

"Grandma does, doesn't she?"

"Yes, I suppose she does," said Bernadette. "I quit going to church after your father left us. I went back the Sunday after my divorce was final, and hardly anyone would speak to me. I figured if I'd done something so bad that God's people wouldn't speak to me, I didn't need to even go anymore."

"Do you think that the way people in church treat you has anything to do with what God thinks? I mean, you couldn't help it if Dad left you and wanted a divorce, could you?"

"Well, I guess I couldn't help it that he left me. I asked for the divorce, but I didn't know anything else to do. He was gone and wasn't coming back. Some people just thought I should wait I guess. I don't really know, but anyway I was embarrassed. Being divorced is just a bad thing for a woman."

"I was wondering if you would consider going to church with me some time," said Jessie.

"I don't know. I haven't been in a long time," said her mother. "We'll see."

That ended their conversation, as the bus had reached their stop.

CHAPTER 19

Jessie had learned that her mother's bitterness over her marriage had left some deep scars, some of which seemed irreparable, so she was not surprised on Sunday when her mother said "No" to her invitation to accompany her to church. It was disappointing, however. Although Cornelia had never gone with Jessie to church, it seemed more difficult for her to go alone that Sunday.

When she boarded the bus to go to church, she thought of Sam and her family, going to their church, which was only about half a mile from her own. *Why do we go to different churches?* Sam seemed to love her church. Jessie wondered what it would be like to go to her church. She knew that wasn't going to happen, but still she thought about it.

When she arrived at her bus stop, Jessie stepped off the bus and headed toward the church. This time she didn't go in the side door. Sunday School was probably over by now. There were people going up the steps into the big limestone building, so Jessie followed them. She really wanted to believe, to have faith that she could get past the sadness of the last few weeks, but she wasn't sure she could. Her mother couldn't seem to either.

Her mother had been hurt badly—by Jessie's father, by Cornelia's death, by the lonely and difficult life of a divorced woman. But Jessie knew that others had been hurt also, and had overcome their bitterness and gone on to lead happy lives. She wanted that kind of strength.

Jessie slipped in a pew in the back of the sanctuary. Dr. Cleverdon welcomed the congregation to the service, and then the music director led them in singing one of Jessie's favorite hymns, "Guide Me, O Thou Great Jehovah." She was pleased when the young woman sitting next to her shared her hymnal.

The next hymn, "A Mighty Fortress Is Our God," was another familiar one, and Jessie noticed a line in the hymn that she had forgotten: "We will not fear, for God hath willed His truth to triumph thro' us. . ." She didn't remember having noticed that before. Just before the sermon, they sang, "All Hail the Power of Jesus' Name."

Jessie looked at her worship bulletin and noticed the title of the sermon, "The Power That God Gives Us." She was interested in learning whether she would feel any power to pull herself out of this deep despair that kept coming back to her.

The pastor stood up and came to the lectern, looking stern in his black suit and tie. "I will be reading from Paul's letter to the Philippians, chapter 4, verses 10-20," he said. Jessie noticed that there was a Bible in the rack in front of her, but she wasn't sure she could find the verses, and he was already beginning to read. She listened as he read. She noticed that Paul said he had learned to be content with whatever he had, or something like that. Well, *she* did not intend to just be content with everything. Some things needed to be changed. Dr. Cleverdon read on, and when he finished, he said, "I want us to focus on verse 13 this morning, 'I can do all things through Christ, which strengtheneth me.' Have you ever thought you just couldn't handle something?"

In her mind Jessie answered "yes," for there were many things she had doubts about and many things she wanted to change. The preacher began by talking about a group of people in Paul's day called "stoics" who tried to learn to accept everything by learning not to care about anything. Paul, however, was explaining that he couldn't do that, but he relied on God to give him the strength to face life's problems. As the pastor talked, Jessie began to see God as all powerful, as someone on whom his followers could rely to help them through difficult times. But one had to have faith in God to be able to do that. She didn't have that faith yet, but she had some hope.

When Dr. Cleverdon finished his sermon, he invited members to sing a song Jessie had not heard before called, "There's a Wideness in God's Mercy." Jessie didn't try to sing with the congregation, but she listened closely to the words. She particularly liked the line that said, "But we make his love too narrow with false limits of our own." She thought of her mother and how she had been judged because of her divorce by people who "made his love too narrow."

At the end of the service, she was glad she had gone to church,

As she turned to leave, the woman who had shared her hymnal said, "I'm Edna. I don't think I've met you. Are you visiting today?"

"Yes. I came once before. I'm Jessie Thompson."

"Welcome to First Baptist Church, Jessie. I hope you'll come back."

"Thank you," said Jessie as she turned to leave. She wanted to get away before the lady asked her anything else. Based on the way she had been treated in Sunday School after revealing that she worked at the shipyards, she had decided to keep that information to herself.

She thanked the pastor for his "fine sermon" as she left and headed for the bus.

Chapter 20

Without Cornelia, Jessie had all but stopped going to the movies and dances with the young people during the fall. She had little interest in going anywhere. She was surprised when she learned that she had been selected as the "Pin-up girl" for her department. The *Sou'Easter* had been featuring one of the girls who had been chosen in each issue of the shipyard newspaper for several months. She had learned about the selection just about a week after they came back after Cornelia's death, and had forgotten all about it.

Jessie's only pleasure these days was reading. She had little time to do anything except work. But she had trouble falling asleep and would awaken tired every morning. She had found that reading books took her mind off her grief and carried her away to another world where she was not so sad. Often she would fall asleep easily after spending some time reading. One Thursday evening she was lying on her bed reading *Heidi* when her mother walked into her room.

"Why didn't you tell me you were chosen for one of the pin-up girls?" Bernadette asked, waving her copy of the *Sou'Easter* in the air.

"Oh, I forgot all about it," Jessie said. "They told me a while ago. But it's not that important." Jessie felt guilty about enjoying things since her sister's death. It seemed like a betrayal.

"I think it is important. I'm proud of you! They must like you to have singled you out like that," said her mother. "Perhaps we should celebrate—maybe go out to eat at the Pink House Restaurant!"

"We don't have to, but I do love that place! Let's see if Chad and Pat might want to go with us. We've hardly had a chance to visit with them since we came back from Cornelia's funeral."

"That's a good idea, but who would keep the kids?" asked Bernadette.

"I didn't think about that. Do you think Linda might keep them? She was saying the other day that she likes to keep children, and she has kept some others sometimes in the early evening," said Jessie.

Jessie asked Linda if she would be interested in keeping the Johnson kids Saturday evening, and she said she would. Then she called Pat and asked her if they wanted to go to the Pink House with them.

"I would love to!" Pat said immediately. "If I can find a sitter."

"Well, I have kind of taken care of that too, I think," said Jessie. "You know Linda, who lives next door to us in the duplex and works at the shipyards?"

"Oh, yes, I've met her a time or two."

"She is willing to keep the kids if you want her to. She babysits for other people a lot, so I just asked her if she would be interested if you needed her and she said yes."

"Oh thank you, Jessie! That's always my problem. The boys are such a handful, but Carol is almost ten and she will be there to help. Sometimes she acts more like their mother than their sister. Of course, Linda's daughter Mary is old enough to help a little too."

"Yes, and Linda's really good with children, so she'll be fine," said Jessie. "Why don't you and Chad just come over around five and then we can go from here?"

"Okay. I'll call Linda and confirm that I'll need her, and tell her what time we'll bring the kids," said Pat.

There was a bit of excitement in the air on Saturday afternoon. None of them were able to afford to go to the Pink House very often, so they all dressed up in their finest clothes. The building was impressive. It was covered with "pink" stucco and was one of Savannah's oldest restaurants. Built in 1771 for James Habersham Jr., it was also one of the few buildings to survive the fire of 1796. The building had been used for several different purposes, but had always been an important historical landmark.

"Is this some special occasion?" asked Chad as they got near the restaurant.

"As a matter of fact, it is," said Bernadette. "Jessie's department chose her for last month's 'pin-up girl' and I am treating her to a special dinner to celebrate."

"Wow! I'm impressed. I didn't see the last issue of the *Sou'Easter*," said Chad.

"I didn't know about it until I got the newsletter," said Bernadette. "She hadn't even told me about it."

"I think we should definitely celebrate," said Pat. "I know you are having a hard time right now, Jessie. I know you're missing your sister, but I think she'd be proud of you. I know she'd want you to celebrate being selected as a 'pin-up girl,' so let's enjoy the evening in memory of Cornelia."

"I just feel so guilty when I feel anything but sadness," said Jessie. "I know what you're saying is true, but I still feel guilty about enjoying anything."

"I know, but Cornelia loved life and she'd want you to enjoy every moment."

"I'll try then," said Jessie.

As they entered through the Greek portico, Jessie noted the familiar old fanlight over the door. It was reassuring. She had heard stories about the ghost of James Habersham Jr. from those who claimed to have had conversations with him in the old building. She didn't exactly believe them, but she loved hearing the stories.

After studying their menus for several minutes, all four of them chose some kind of seafood for their entrees. Jessie felt as if she were in a dream world. Not only was the food delicious, but the atmosphere was magical. The waiters were professional and especially knowledgeable about both the restaurant and the food.

When they had almost finished their meal, the waiter asked about desserts, and Chad said, "Of course!" Although Jessie was stuffed, she selected their peach cobbler. The other three chose the chocolate cake. Dessert was a real treat, with the sugar rationing causing few desserts to be eaten, especially at home.

Driving home that evening, Jessie was grateful for her cousins and their willingness to go to dinner with them. It helped that Chad and Pat seemed to understand the difficulty she was having, yet they gently encouraged her to get back into the world and live.

When they got home, Linda met them at the door and put her finger to her lips, signaling them that the twins were asleep. Carol was reading a story to Mary in her bedroom, and she was almost asleep too.

"We had a wonderful evening," said Linda. "The boys are so cute, and so well-behaved. We played in the yard, and they are probably filthy dirty, but I think they had a good time."

"Thank you so much. I hope you are not exhausted. They're a handful sometimes," said Pat.

"No," said Linda. "They were fine. And Carol is so much help. She knows everything about what they need, and she was also very good with Mary. Mary loves to have someone read to her, and Carol is such a good reader."

"Well, maybe we can do it again sometime. I often need someone, especially with John and Mack. It's hard to take them anywhere when I'm by myself—and I'm often by myself because Chad works long hours." She picked up one of the boys, and Chad took the other. Carol came out of Mary's room smiling.

"Okay. Is everybody ready to go?" asked Chad. "We enjoyed it, Miss Pin-up Girl," he said, looking at Jessie.

"Me too," she said.

After that evening Jessie visited often with Linda, and she and her mother spent time with Chad and Pat on the weekends. Jessie even kept the kids for them a few times when they needed her. Due to her schedule though, she had little time to do anything other than work. She still had no interest in going to dances or to the Lucas Theater to see movies. It reminded her too much of Cornelia.

CHAPTER 21

Despite Jessie's frustration with some of the men who didn't think women could do jobs usually reserved for men, she often found herself assuming that somewhere in her future she would be a wife and mother. Just what was the role of women in this world? She often wondered what had happened to Al. Would he come back some day and want to marry her? Would she want to be a wife?

One day she asked her friend Sam what she thought about it. "Oh, not me. I don't want to be a wife to anyone. I just want to be a doctor. It's too much trouble to be a wife and mother. I'll have enough trouble just achieving my own goals without dragging a husband along with me."

"But what if you fall in love with someone?" asked Jessie.

"I won't," replied Sam.

"If I fall in love, I might get married," said Jessie.

"That's all right," assured Sam. "But I'm not."

"Couldn't you do both? Couldn't you be a good doctor *and* a good wife?"

"I don't think I could. This whole idea of being committed to someone else and meeting all their needs is just not for me." She stopped. "Maybe, being white, you could do that, but I couldn't."

Jessie pondered what Sam had said. Was it a cultural thing? Did it really matter what color you were? She didn't think so, but she did see that the role of women seemed to be changing. She questioned Sam, "Do you think it's a good thing for women to work in jobs usually held by men?"

"Yes, I do. Why can't we do anything they can?"

"I think that too, but sometimes I wonder if we can do everything and still have a family."

"Men have always had a choice about what they do, but women have been expected to stay home with the kids," said Sam.

"It's just so weird. On the one hand, men here are often critical of us and act like we don't know what we're doing. But everywhere you look in town there are advertisements directed toward women, wanting them to work for the government and take up the slack while the men are gone to war."

"I guess the government wants women to work, but the actual men workers don't think we can do it," proposed Sam.

"I suppose so," agreed Jessie. "I saw a bunch of signs yesterday. One read, 'Do the job he left behind.' Another one had the word 'women' and a huge picture of where all these women were working, and it read 'There's work to be done and a war to be won . . . NOW.' All of them indicate they want women workers. But you know, I haven't seen any new signs lately."

"I haven't seen any new ones either. I saw an advertisement last year for the Westinghouse Corporation that had this girl (white of course)," Sam said, smiling. "She was holding up her arm, like she was showing her muscles, and it said, 'We Can Do It!'—I liked it because a lot of the men think we can't."

"I think women have made a great effort to help win the war, and I think that picture is right—We *can* do it," said Jessie.

Cornelia's death had forced Jessie to grow up a little. When they moved to Savannah, she had become "Cornelia's little sister" to all of their friends. Although Jessie had the same training and did much of the same work, she had become dependent on Cornelia in many ways, especially in their social activities. Cornelia decided when, where, and with whom they went to the movies or dancing. Now she had no one to guide her. She enjoyed talking to Sam at lunch, but she knew that she and Sam could not really be friends or do things together outside of work. Even there, she was derided for talking to Sam. It would be completely unacceptable outside of work.

One day as she was leaving work, she saw her next-door neighbor Linda coming out at the same time. Linda saw her too and waved. "I haven't seen you in a few days," said Linda.

"I know," agreed Jessie. "It's funny how we can work at the same place and seldom see each other."

"I usually get off a little earlier so I can pick up Mary at the daycare place," said Linda. "Today I had to work later because we are trying to finish up a job on the hot ship this week."

"When does it launch?" asked Jessie.

"I don't know—but soon, Friday maybe." They walked along together.

Jessie looked at Linda. She looked tired. "Do you ever get to go out, or anything?"

"Not really," said Linda. "I have to be away from Mary all day, so I usually stay home with her when I'm not working."

Bernadette was walking along with one of her coworkers several steps ahead of them. Jessie said, "Maybe she could stay with Mama one evening, and you and I could go out to eat or something."

"That would be great if she could," said Linda. "Mary likes your mother. I can't leave her with just anyone, especially since she's at daycare all the time when I work. Next year she'll be in school. Maybe I will feel differently then."

"I'll talk to Mama and see what she says," Jessie promised. She and her mother had never heard Linda mention a husband. By this time it was obvious there wasn't one, but they had no idea what her situation was.

Friday evening after dinner, Jessie said, "Mama, I talked to Linda on the way home today."

"Really? I don't think I've ever seen her at work or afterwards," said Bernadette.

"I hadn't either. I think most of the time she leaves at a different time to pick up Mary at daycare. Today she was working on the hot ship, so she had to be there a little later. I feel sorry for her. I don't think she ever gets to go out and do anything fun for herself."

"I understand that. It was that way when Dan first left me. You and Cornelia were three and five."

"Is she divorced, or what happened to Mary's dad?" asked Jessie.

"I don't know. But don't ask her about it unless she brings it up. I used to hate it when people asked about Dan."

"I won't. I was just wondering whether you might keep Mary tomorrow night and let Linda and me go out to eat, just to give her a break."

"Sure. Mary is so sweet. If I have any sugar, I might let her help me make some cookies," said Bernadette.

"Great. I just worry about Linda having to work all the time and not getting to do anything fun. She said that she hated leaving Mary again after being at work all week, but she trusts you, and if she spends tomorrow with Mary she won't feel so bad about leaving her for a while in the evening. I'll go tell her."

Jessie got up and went next door. When Linda came to the door Jessie said, "It's all set. You and I are going out on the town tomorrow evening."

Linda's face lit up. "Great! Where are we going?"

"Let's go to Johnny Harris. I haven't been there in a while. We might even find a soldier who would dance with us!" Jessie smiled. "Put on your best party dress."

"I will!" said Linda. "I haven't done that in a long time."

As Jessie headed back to her place, her smile disappeared and in its place her lips formed a thin line of determination. When she told her mother their plan, Bernadette smiled. "I am so glad you've decided to get out and do something fun. You know, Linda isn't the only one who hasn't been going out lately. You are young and need to enjoy it while you can."

"I guess you're right," she said, sighing as she went to her room.

The next evening Jessie tried on three different dresses before she settled on the newest one: black satin. The neck line was lower in the back. She put on her new shoes she had bought using the rationing coupon and twirled around as if she were dancing. She thought of the many young girls who would have to wear their cardboard shoes and the soldiers who might not have what they needed because of the lack of leather. Well, Jessie decided there was nothing she could do about that.

Even after all her preparation for the evening, Jessie was anxious. It was the first time she had gone to such an event without Cornelia by her side. She didn't talk much on the bus ride.

"Are you all right?" asked Linda, as they exited the bus.

"Yes. I'm fine," she said, taking a deep breath.

"You don't seem fine," said Linda. "You look like you're scared or something."

"It's just that I haven't been anywhere like this without Cornelia," Jessie added.

"Oh, of course," said Linda. "I'm sorry that I didn't think about how you must feel. I know it's got to be difficult for you. I can't replace your sister, but I hope I can be of help if you need anything."

"Thank you. I don't need anything. Things are just so different now. I always depended on her so much. It wasn't that she actually did anything. It was more like my identity was 'Cornelia's little sister.' It's hard to explain."

"I understand a little of what that feels like," confided Linda. "I've not said anything about it, but when my husband left me, it was sort of like that. I worked while he was in medical school, and then we moved to Macon, where he joined a medical practice not long after Mary was born. My identity was completely tied up in being a doctor's wife. I thought everything was fine until I learned that he was having an affair with his nurse. When I confronted him, he actually seemed relieved that I had learned about it. He told me he wanted a divorce so he could marry her—and just like that, I was single again!"

"Oh, I am so sorry. That must have been terrible," said Jessie.

"It was, and still is in some ways. But you know, it wasn't my fault. I gave our marriage my all. But he didn't, and he's the loser, because he is missing out on all the wonderful things our daughter is learning and doing. I'm getting to enjoy all that."

"How did you decide to work in Savannah?" asked Jessie.

"After the divorce I stayed on in Macon for a while because my parents were not too far away. But like I said, I had always just been 'the wife of Doctor Hawkins' and I needed to figure out who I was. When I saw an advertisement wanting workers at Southeastern, I decided to give it a try."

"My mother says when the war is over, we'll probably have to do something else. What are your plans if they don't need us any more after the war?"

"Oh, I took this job because it pays good, but I'm saving to go to school. Mary's father sends child support, so I don't have too many expenses. I hope to have enough saved to go to college. I didn't get but one year of college before I dropped out to help my husband through medical school."

"What did you do?" asked Jessie.

"I worked in a doctor's office—not my husband's office, though. I think I'd like to be a nurse, so I'll probably go to nurses' training."

"I think you'd make a good one."

When they arrived at the restaurant there was already a good crowd, but Jessie and Linda were seated almost immediately. Jessie thought back to the last time she ate there with Al. Cornelia had been there with her friend too. It took her a few minutes to stop reminiscing. Linda seemed to understand about Jessie sitting there quietly, taking it all in. Then the waiter came for their drink orders, and Jessie and Linda began discussing the menu.

The evening was nice and Jessie enjoyed the food, but as they entered the dance floor looking around for a soldier who was seeking a dance partner, Jessie's face was solemn. She watched as Linda began a conversation with one of the young men. They talked for a moment, and then they looked toward Jessie. Linda motioned for Jessie to come over. As she walked over, another young man approached them. He looked slightly familiar.

"Jessie, this is Jack," Linda said.

Jack shook her hand and then looked at his friend. "And this is David," he said.

"Aren't you a friend of Al Donaldson's?" David asked.

"Yes! Do you know him?" asked Jessie.

"I sure do," he said. "We grew up together, were in basic training together, and we've been on leave here at the same time. I thought I recognized you!"

David and Jessie danced several times that evening, and she relaxed some. She told him about Al's plans to visit his family at Christmas. She also told him about her sister's death. The evening was better than she had expected, and she suspected it was better than Linda expected it to be also.

When they were leaving, David said, "Thank you for making us feel at home in Savannah tonight. It's sometimes difficult when we're on leave a few days to find someone who is willing just to talk—and to dance with, of course."

"Yes," Jack chimed in. "I have laughed more than I have in a month. It's good to get a chance to relax during all this serious war business."

"We enjoyed it too," the girls said as they turned to leave.

Although Linda was several years older than Jessie, they got along well. When they returned home, Jessie's mother had put Mary to bed and was reading a magazine. "How did it go? Did she drive you crazy?" asked Linda.

"Oh, we had a great time. She was no trouble at all. We stayed at my place until after we ate. Then we came over here, and I turned on the radio and found some music. She pretended she was at Johnny Harris' ballroom, dancing. She may be an entertainer some day!"

Jessie talked to her mother for a while before she went to her room and read a few more chapters in *Heidi*. As she read, the story carried her away to the faraway country of Switzerland. Before long, her eyes began to droop and she laid the book down beside her and drifted off to sleep.

CHAPTER 22

Knowing that Al planned to spend Christmas with his family, Jessie did not expect to hear from him during December. She was surprised to get a phone call from him one chilly Saturday morning.

"I just got home for a few days and decided to give you a call," he said. "I had hoped to be here on Christmas Day, but I have to return before then."

"I'm sorry. I know you were looking forward to it."

"It's really not a problem. We're just going to celebrate early before I leave," Al said.

"Good. So what's the weather like there?" asked Jessie.

"It's cold here right now—about 30 degrees—and they're predicting snow tonight."

"It seldom gets that cold here, and we hardly ever have snow. What part of Oklahoma are you in?"

"Up in the northwest corner, near the panhandle—between Buffalo and Beaver."

"Are you enjoying being with your family? I guess that is a silly question—of course you are," said Jessie.

"Yes, I am. Listen, David told me about your sister Cornelia. I was so sorry to hear about that," said Al. "I know this is a hard time for you and your mother."

"It's been very difficult for us both," said Jessie. "I really appreciate your calling. That means a lot to me."

"I'm sorry I can't come to see you, but just know that I am thinking about you and hoping you can get through this Christmas," he said.

"Thank you. Thank you so much. I really needed that encouragement."

"Will you and your mother be going back to Alabama at Christmas?"

"No. We'll stay here. We only have the weekend and Monday off work, so we just couldn't go. We may get together with my mother's cousin on Christmas Day."

"That's good. I forgot that you have cousins in Savannah. That will be good for you and your mother," said Al.

"Also, my grandmother might get to come here for a few days. My mother's brother and his wife might bring her, but we don't know for sure yet."

"I hope that works out. I have to go now, but I wanted to talk to you after David told me about your sister," said Al.

"Thank you for calling, and you have a good Christmas with your family," said Jessie before she hung up. She sat there for a while, thinking back over their talk. She couldn't believe Al had called her. According to her mother, most men weren't very thoughtful.

Every time she talked to Al, she realized it could be her last time to hear his voice. It was not a morbid thought, but she just knew it was a possibility, so she listened carefully. Al's voice was soft, but she could hear and understand him easily. It was kind of musical. Something about it reminded Jessie of the song that was getting so popular by Bing Crosby and the Andrew Sisters called "Don't Fence Me In." When the song played right after the news that night, she thought of Al's voice.

Every night just before the news, Bernadette would take out a map that showed all the different places where the men were fighting. She would place it on the table and use a foot ruler to point to all the places they talked about. A few days after Al had called, the reporter talked about the heavy fighting in Belgium, and mentioned foreign-sounding names such as Ardennes and Luxembourg along with Germany. Jessie and her mother stood over the table and looked at each of the locations on the big map. It sounded like a huge battle.

The announcer said, "They're calling it the 'Battle of the Bulge' because it is a bulge in the battle lines." It sounded like the largest battle they'd fought, and yet the Allies had gained much ground in the last few months. Jessie looked at the map and wondered where Al would be when he returned in a few days. He had talked about flowers, and grass, and beautiful mountains in one of his letters, but now it was winter, and according to the announcer it was extremely cold in Belgium.

During December, Jessie spent time with Chad and his family and Linda next door, and she and her mother went through the motions of getting ready for Christmas. They found some small toys for each of the Johnson children and for Linda's little Mary. Jessie smiled as she wrapped the baby dolls for Mary and Carol and the puzzle for John and the airplane for Mack. The twins were very different.

She thought the puzzle was especially right for John, who was more serious and loved puzzles. Mack, on the other hand, noticed every airplane that flew over. Linda had gone with Jessie to help select the children's gifts.

On Tuesday evening before Christmas the following Monday, Chad brought a Christmas tree to Jessie and Bernadette and relayed a message: "Pat said to tell you that she wants you to come for lunch around one o'clock on Christmas Day, but we wanted you to have a tree to enjoy this week so we got an extra one."

"We don't even have decorations for a tree," said Bernadette, sighing. Last year, they had decided not to get into decorating since they were going to Chad and Pat's for Christmas Day and they had already spent a good bit of money that fall just getting settled into a new place.

"That's not a problem," said Chad. "Pat and I had a bunch of decorations we haven't used since the twins came along, so I've brought them to you. Of course you can add some if you want to, but there are enough here for a start." He stepped out to his car and retrieved a box of decorations and then returned to the house.

Chad probably knew this Christmas was difficult, thought Jessie. "That's great," she said. "Thank you so much." He helped them put the tree up and stayed and helped them hang the few ornaments. The women found some red ribbon in the closet and draped it around the tree also. When they finished, it looked festive if not elaborate. Jessie went into her room and brought the four gifts she had wrapped for the children and laid them under the tree.

After Chad left, Bernadette went into her room and stayed for some time. Jessie sat and looked at the tree and remembered former Christmases when she and Cornelia had run into the living room gleefully on Christmas morning to enjoy a new toy and a piece of fruit or a candy bar. In her mind she could hear the laughter and smell the aroma of cinnamon buns baking in her grandmother's oven.

Jessie had been conflicted about how to handle gifts this year. Neither she nor her mother had much enthusiasm about Christmas presents. She wasn't sure her mother had even bought her anything. When she was shopping with Linda for the children, however, she saw a sweater in Adler's Department Store that she remembered her mother admiring. It was practical, not fancy, but she decided to buy it for her mother for Christmas. She wasn't sure whether she would give it to her at home or at the Johnsons, but she wanted to have it for when it was the right time.

That evening Pat called. When Jessie answered the phone, Pat said, "I forgot to tell Chad to invite Linda and Mary to come for lunch on Monday also if they are free."

"I will check with Linda and call you back in a while," said Jessie. "I think they'll be here. She has not said anything about going anywhere." As soon as they hung up, Jessie went next door and asked Linda if they could eat with the Johnsons on Monday.

"I can," she said. "I'll have to check to see what time Mary's dad is picking her up that afternoon." She stepped out the door so Mary wouldn't hear her. "It's interesting how he made this big deal about getting her on Christmas Day, but when it came down to making plans, he and his wife seemed almost too busy to fool with her. It makes me angry sometimes. But again, I get more time with her, so I'm not complaining."

Jessie reported back to Pat before the evening was over. With each day of the week before Christmas, Jessie felt terrible sadness sweeping over her with increasing intensity. She knew it was the same for her mother, but they didn't talk about it. It was just there. On Saturday, Linda mentioned to Jessie and Bernadette that she and Mary had been attending a small church outside of town the last few months and that they were having a Christmas program that night. "The children present the program, and Mary asked if you and your mother might come," she said to Jessie.

"I will ask Mother, but I think so."

At first Bernadette seemed reluctant, saying something about not being sure she could handle it, but finally she agreed to go. The little white church was bursting with excitement when they entered. Linda said they would sing carols and then the older children would present a play, followed by the younger ones, including Mary, giving their part of the program. "I've practiced for a long time," Mary said. "We act out each line, and I know exactly what to do." She began to recite a line or two and show them what actions went with which lines.

"Shhhh," said her mother as the program began.

After leading the congregation in singing "Joy to the World" and several other familiar carols, the song leader called on one of the children's workers to introduce the program. The lady came to the front of the room and said that the children's choir would present a play called "No Room in the Inn."

A curtain covered the front of the stage until she announced the title of the play. Then the curtains opened to an empty stage. A young man and woman (two children actually) appeared from the right, dressed in what looked like bathrobes. They proceeded across the stage to the left, where a man was standing on the other side of a window. Jessie listened as the couple explained their need for a place for their baby to be born, and were told of course that "There is no room in the inn." As the play progressed, the scene changed from the inn to the stable, where the baby appeared in the manger, and later the shepherds and wise men came.

The story was familiar because Jessie had heard it read from the second chapter of Luke several times at Christmas. The shepherds bowed down and worshipped the baby Jesus, and the Wise Men brought him gold, frankincense, and myrrh. Jessie had never understood the significance of the two last gifts, but she could appreciate the gold.

The play ended soon after that, and it was probably a good thing since some of the younger children were about to fall asleep and the others were getting restless. After the actors and actresses took their bows and received their deserved applause, the workers with the younger children began gathering them to the side of the stage to begin their part of the program. Unlike some of the younger children who were clinging tightly to their mothers in tears, Mary marched right up to the front with her teacher, ready to take her place on the stage.

"I hope she doesn't embarrass us all by drawing attention to herself," Linda whispered to Jessie. About that time, Mary looked straight at them, smiled and waved her arm.

"The children will sing two carols and act them out as they sing," said their leader, marching all ten of the children onto the stage. Jessie wondered what the chances were that all ten of the four- and five-year-olds would do the same actions at the same time. As soon as they began singing "Silent Night," it was obvious that the little boy next to Mary had no idea what he was supposed to do. It was also obvious that Mary noticed it.

When they got to the line "Holy infant so tender and mild" Mary poked him in the ribs and motioned to him to do what she was doing. Of course, it was too late. All the way through the song Mary got more frustrated with the child.

By the time they got to their second song, "Away in a Manger," it was clear that Mary was pondering what she could do to get the boy back on track. She was probably remembering what her teacher had done during practice. When they got to the line, "The baby awakes," he was still in "sleeping" mode.

"Stop!" Mary yelled. Everyone stopped. The director looked perplexed. Linda gasped.

Mary faced the little boy and put her hands on her hips. "Bobby, when we sing 'the baby awakes' you're supposed to wake up! Pay attention next time and do that, okay?"

Bobby nodded his head and grinned. Mary got back in line, looked at the teacher and they began the verse again, and this time Bobby woke up at the proper time. The audience unsuccessfully tried to stifle their laughter and Linda shook her head, not knowing whether to laugh or cry. Afterwards, she apologized to the little boy's mother, but his mother said, "Well, she was right. He wasn't paying attention."

"We enjoyed your program," said Jessie and her mother on the way home.

"Thank you," said Mary quietly. "It would have been better if Bobby had known all the actions, but he had only been there a few times, so I guess he didn't."

Jessie controlled her urge to laugh, knowing that Linda probably didn't want to encourage Mary in trying to take over the director's job.

"Well, I thought it was a wonderful program. Thank you for inviting us," said Bernadette. When they got home, Jessie and her mother had the best laugh they'd had in a long time. Before they went to bed, Jessie asked, "Mama, do you want to go to church with me tomorrow?"

"Maybe," said Bernadette. "I'll see how I feel in the morning."

"I'd love for you to go with me. I think you'd like Dr. Cleverdon."

On Sunday morning Bernadette decided to go with Jessie to church. As Dr. Cleverdon read the Christmas story from the book of Luke, Jessie poked her mother and grinned as they remembered little Mary and the program the night before. Focusing on the idea of God coming into the world in unusual ways, the pastor made the point that sometimes we may not recognize God's coming because we are too busy with our own worries and cares to see him. Jessie thought that was a message she and her mother really needed as they worked through their grief for her sister. Maybe they needed to look for the ways in which God was working in their world, even as they grieved. Christmas Eve turned out to be a peaceful, if not exciting, day.

When Jessie awoke on Monday morning, she remembered it was Christmas Day. As usual, her first thought as she looked around the room was that she was alone—Cornelia was gone. Her next thought was the gift she had wrapped earlier for her mother. In case her mother didn't plan to exchange gifts with her, she decided it would be better to go ahead and give it to her before they went to lunch at Chad's. She retrieved the package from her closet and made her way toward the kitchen where she heard her mother making breakfast.

As she looked into the living room at the tree, she noticed a new package lying near the back of the children's gifts. So her mother *had* bought her a gift—or maybe it was for the Johnsons. Anyway, at least she had done some Christmas shopping. She ran over and placed her package under the tree, and as she did she saw her name on the extra gift she had seen. Quietly she entered the kitchen as her mother turned around.

"Merry Christmas, Mama," said Jessie.

"And to you, Dear," said Bernadette.

After breakfast, Bernadette said, "I got you a little gift. Do you want to open it now, or do you want to open it at Chad's later?"

"Now! I got you one too!"

"Really?" said her mother. "I had no idea you had bought me a gift."

"I didn't know you had got me one either," said Jessie. "I guess we both had the same idea though."

When Jessie opened her package, she realized it was a sweater she had admired the day they went shopping. So they had both really had a similar idea!

When the Thompsons and Linda and Mary arrived at the Johnsons' home, everything was focused on the kids. John and Mack were so excited they could hardly contain themselves, and they had to show everyone all the things Santa had brought them. Carol was excited too, although she was a little more reserved than the twins. Jessie was glad she had made the effort to purchase toys.

John tried to put his wooden puzzle pieces together as soon as he opened his box, while Mack "zoom-zoomed" his airplane all around the living room. Carol took Mary back to her room where she had other dolls and doll clothes to entertain them. Although Carol was a good bit older, she still enjoyed dressing and undressing the dolls and showing Mary her toys.

Pat loved to cook, and she was excited to have a big group to enjoy her efforts. "This is the best turkey I've ever tasted," said Linda.

"She had to get up before daylight to get it baked," said Chad, pride in his voice.

"I saw some fruitcake in there, too," said Jessie. "I love your fruitcake."

"I had to do some 'cajoling' to get enough sugar for the dessert," said Chad. "We didn't have quite enough for the cake and the apple pie, but our neighbor wasn't cooking today, so she let us borrow some of her stamps."

"I am so glad she did," said Linda. "We haven't had anything sweet for weeks."

"Why did they ration sugar?" asked Jessie.

"They need it for the soldiers," said Chad. "We, on the other hand, are not as important." He smiled at Jessie.

"But I need sweets too," she said. "What about me?"

"You'll just have to adjust." He laughed as he pointed at her.

It was late in the afternoon before the women finished cleaning up after lunch and began to get ready to leave.

"Tomorrow morning will be here before we know it," said Bernadette. "After three days off, I'm dreading going back to work."

"Me too," said Linda and Jessie at the same time.

"Can I stay with Carol?" asked Mary. "We're having fun."

"I'm sorry, honey," said Linda. "But we have to go now. Carol needs to get her sleep and get ready to go back to school too."

Mary followed her mother out of the room with a frown.

"Maybe you can come back to play again sometime soon," said Pat.

Linda and the Thompsons thanked the Johnsons again for inviting them to come for Christmas lunch and then headed home.

CHAPTER 23

As Jessie and her mother listened to the news the next evening, the "Battle of the Bulge" still seemed the focus of attention. Jessie wondered if Al was in Belgium or France or somewhere near the fighting. She knew that it was likely he was involved in that area since he had been required to go back to work early. She worried about the pressure he was under, knowing that the stress of his work had caused him to lose his hair. She looked forward to receiving her usual letter from him by the end of the week.

By Wednesday it was getting colder, and by Thursday it had begun to rain as Jessie arrived and checked in to work. She had worn warmer clothes, but the rain made it seem colder than usual. She remembered the winter before when she had sat on a piece of cardboard to avoid being so cold, and then spending a day or so at home sick.

Huddled in the shelter the hot ship provided at lunch, Sam looked up as Jessie took out her peanut butter sandwich from her lunch bag. "Have you heard from your bomber boyfriend this week?" she asked.

"Not yet, but I didn't expect to before tomorrow since it's Christmas week. I may not even hear at all this week." Jessie sighed. "I worry about him. I heard that the bombers are more vulnerable than any other servicemen. They have to fly during the day to identify their targets, and that makes it easy for them to be shot down. I hate to even think about it."

"I know. But they are heroes too. I'm sure you're proud to know him."

"I am. I just hope he comes home safe and sound."

"Do you remember that time we talked about our plans and whether we would get married and have a family?" asked Sam.

"Yes and you didn't seem interested in that life at all," responded Jessie.

"I know. And I'm still not, but I have thought about it, and someday I might," said Sam. "I guess my point was, and is, that in my case I'll do well to just get in college and work toward becoming a doctor. I may not even make it. But I have to make that my one goal. I can't worry about chasing other goals until I achieve that one." Sam looked at Jessie. "I'm not sure you realize how different it is for a black girl. Becoming a doctor is just unheard of. My brother just laughs at me for even thinking I could do that."

"Well, he shouldn't laugh at you." Jessie laughed. "Someday you can laugh at him for not believing in you!"

"I hope that will be the case, but who knows? I'm not giving up any time soon though."

"Where do you plan to go to college and medical school?" asked Jessie.

"The University of Illinois," answered Sam without hesitation.

Jessie raised her eyebrows. "Really? Why?"

"Well, I read about a woman. Her name was Helen Dickens, and she earned a medical degree there. She was the only black woman in her class. That was about ten years ago, but that proves it can be done."

"Yes, it does. How would you pay for it?"

"I don't know. It may take me a long time. I have a cousin who lives there. I may see if I could go up there and live and work until I have enough money to go to school. I don't know."

"Don't give up on it. I believe you'll do it!"

"Thank you for believing in me," said Sam. "That means a lot."

"How could I not believe in you?" said Jessie. "You have so much drive, and you have much more to overcome. I am just so anxious to get through all this war stuff and get back to school. I don't really know for sure how I can pay for school and all that. But you, you have all the prejudice to overcome in addition to what I have, and yet you're so determined. You make me want to make something of myself."

"And you will," said Sam, picking up her lunch pail. "We'd better get back to work."

As she picked up her gloves and retrieved her welding equipment after lunch, Jessie was thankful for her gloves and helmet that had been so hot and cumbersome a few months ago. Even her heavy boots felt good in the cold rain. Nevertheless, trying to keep her rod steady as she welded throughout the afternoon left her hands and arms tired and achy by the end of her shift, and she was glad to head home. Her mother seemed exhausted too.

Despite the fact that she had told Sam she might not hear from Al that week, the first thing she did when she arrived home was check the mail. No letter. When the news came on at six and they mentioned a bomber that had gone down, she couldn't help wondering if Al was in it.

"Do you want to go to the movies tomorrow night?" Jessie asked Linda. "Mom said Mary could stay with her."

"Sure," said Linda. "What's on?"

"*Arsenic and Old Lace.*"

"I've heard that's hilarious," said Linda. "I've been wanting to see it. It's based on the Broadway comedy I think—maybe sort of dark but funny also."

"Let's get there in time for the newsreel," said Jessie. "I want to see what they're saying about the war."

"You're worried about Al, aren't you?" said Linda.

"Yes, I am. I know he probably just hasn't had time to write since Christmas, but still—" Jessie hesitated. "I guess I've been used to hearing from him about every week."

When she and her mother got home, Jessie mentioned Al and the letter she had not received.

"Men don't think like women do," said her mother. "He has probably just forgotten about writing."

"Maybe," said Jessie. "I hope that's it."

Friday evening Linda and Jessie arrived at the Lucas Theater in plenty of time to hear the advertisements about buying war bonds and other promotional announcements regarding the war and then the newsreel coming straight from the battle front. They made it sound like the United States was winning along the Belgium/France border, but at the same time the news clips of soldiers on the ground and snow-covered forests of the Ardennes made Jessie shudder. After a few minutes her stomach grew tight; she wanted to get out of the theater. Just as she was about to tell Linda she would have to go, they finished the news and began to show advertisements for popcorn and Cracker Jacks.

Arsenic and Old Lace was both funny and "evil," as Linda put it. The highlight for Linda and Jessie, of course, was seeing Cary Grant play Mortimer, the two old ladies' nephew.

By the end of the first week in January, Jessie was beginning to get worried about Al. She still had not received a letter, and although she knew there were times he might not be able to write, she also knew that the B-17 bombers were always in the middle of the battles and that some had been shot down by the Germans. With every week, she became more anxious. She read the newspaper every chance she got, and listened to the evening news every night.

"Listen," said Jessie's mother one evening in mid-January. "It sounds like the battle in Belgium may be over." She turned up the radio as the announcer continued.

"General Patton's maneuvering of the Third Army to Bastogne proved vital to the allied defense, leading to the neutralization of the German counteroffensive despite heavy casualties."

All Jessie heard was "despite heavy casualties." Her heart sank.

The announcer continued with the update, and Jessie went into her room and cried.

Despite the fact that the Battle of the Bulge seemed to be over, fighting continued over the next few weeks—and still no word from Al. At first Jessie thought there might be a way she could contact his family, but she had no idea what any of their names were. Also, she wasn't sure she wanted to do that. What if they had received word of his death? What could she say to them? And what if they hadn't heard? Did they even know that she was his friend? In the end, she just kept waiting.

Chapter 24

At the shipyard there was some talk of the war in Europe coming to an end, and Jessie was beginning to think she might be getting back to school that fall. Her mother had even mentioned the possibility that if they were still in Savannah, she might be able to finish high school there. Things were still uncertain though. As there was talk of the war winding down in Europe, the U.S. Marines invaded the island of Iwo Jima in February. The news reporter spoke of a "fierce battle" as they listened to the evening news. It did not sound like things were coming to a close to Jessie.

"Why can't they just quit fighting?" she said to her mother. "It's getting old. I'm tired of all this dying." She wondered if Al was dead.

Every evening after work they would listen to the news and look at their big map. They had left it out on the table, exposing it to coffee splatters and food crumbs, but they could still read it—most of it anyway.

Throughout March they had hardly missed a night pinpointing every place that was mentioned on the news. On March 22 it was Oppenheim, Germany. General Patton sneaked a division of his U.S. Third Army across the Rhine at Oppenheim. According to the news, this was a major blow to Hitler and his supporters. Jessie didn't want to hear about it but didn't want to miss it either. The fact was, the news was making Jessie depressed. She still missed Cornelia, she thought Al had probably been killed in battle, and she had no idea where any of her friends back in Alabama were or what they were doing. She felt like she was sinking into a hole with no way out. She had kept hoping to hear that the war was over and she could go home, but it seemed as if that wasn't going to happen any time soon.

"I don't want to hear the news," she said to her mother the first of April. "I'm going to my room and read *Little Women*. Tell me if there's anything I really need to know."

"Okay," said her mother as she turned on the radio and went over to the map on the table.

Jessie went into her room and immersed herself in the lives of Meg, Jo, Beth, and Amy. She had always known about Louisa May Alcott's *Little Women*, but had never known that she had lots in common with the characters. She was fascinated that the girls lived in a home without a father's presence, it was a war time, and the girls had to work to help with expenses—just like she did. But they didn't have a radio! During the next week Jessie continued to opt for reading each evening while the newscaster told all the gory details of the war. She felt better that week, and her mother seldom mentioned what was happening in the news.

On Thursday, April 12, however, her mother burst into her room almost as soon as Jessie closed her door and practically shouted, "Jessie, you must come listen to this!"

The first words Jessie heard as she entered the kitchen were "President Roosevelt died soon after in Warm Springs, Georgia." They listened as the reporter continued to give details about what was happening.

"Did they say what happened to him?" Jessie asked her mother when he finished.

"Apparently he had a cerebral hemorrhage. They said he grabbed his head and fell over."

"What will we do without a president?" asked Jessie.

"Vice-president Truman will be sworn in immediately," said Bernadette. "It may have already been done."

"But with the war going on, will he know what to do?"

"That's a good question. I don't know much about him, but I guess he's been working with President Roosevelt."

For the next few days the news was mostly about the president's death, funeral plans, and who said what about the new president. Jessie got back into the habit of joining her mother each evening for the six o'clock news. At work and in the street the talk turned from the battles to the death of the president.

Then on April 30, 1945, there was more shocking news: Adolph Hitler had committed suicide! The news reporter said that as it became increasingly clear to Hitler that his troops were losing the battle, he burrowed away in a refurbished air-raid shelter, consumed a cyanide capsule, and shot himself with a pistol. According to reporters, he had been warned by officers that the Russians were only a day or so from overtaking him, and was advised to escape to Berchtesgaden, a small town in the Bavarian Alps where he owned a home. Instead, he committed suicide. It was reported that his new wife, Eva Braun, had also poisoned herself.

Linda and Jessie decided to go to the movies on Friday night to see *Going My Way* with Bing Crosby. It was the first weekend in May, and in view of all the upheaval in the news due to the death of the president and later Hitler's suicide, they needed a break from the war news. They had not intended to get there in time for the newsreel before the movie, but as they walked into the theater, it was still on. The news clips came from somewhere in Italy, and they were talking about the "Po Valley Campaign," which had ended on May 2. They were showing some rugged mountain terrain, but the newsreel was almost finished. Jessie was glad.

The music in the film carried Jessie away from all the war stories as she listened to Bing Crosby and the boys' choir singing everything from "Swinging on a Star" to "Three Blind Mice."

"That was a fine movie," commented Jessie as they left the theater.

"The best," said Linda, "and an excellent way to end our week."

On Monday afternoon Jessie was busy welding when she heard a commotion and then someone with a megaphone making an announcement: "We have just heard that Germany has surrendered to the Allies. General Alfred Jodl, representing the German High Command, signed the unconditional surrender of both east and west forces in Reims, France, which will take effect tomorrow."

The shipyard had obviously begun to cut back on the production of Liberty Ships, and many people recommended that workers, especially women, would need to prepare for other work. This news really put the shipyard abuzz with speculation about what would happen during the summer. In fact, they had cut back from three shifts to two in April, but with the thousands of workers, Jessie hardly noticed.

"I have applied at Sears and I'm leaving this place," said one of Jessie's coworkers. "I can't wait around until I'm fired. I have a wife and two kids to support."

The next day at lunch Jessie asked Sam, "Have you thought about what you'll do when you can no longer work here? It sounds like this place might be shutting down before too long if the war really ends."

"I'll just go back and finish school I guess," said Sam. "I'm working until they throw me out, though, 'cause I need the money!"

"Same here, except I'm not sure whether I'll finish school here or go back to Alabama. Mama has been thinking about staying on in Savannah. If she does, I might go to school here."

Sam was quiet for a moment. "Nothing official has been said about shutting this place down yet, has it?"

"I don't think so. Of course they have cut out one of the shifts," said Jessie. "Why do you ask?"

"I just wondered. My people will probably be cut out first."

"We will probably all be here for a while," said Jessie.

"I hope so," said Sam. "I really need to work a while longer."

Jessie sensed that the idea of losing her job made Sam especially anxious. They had never talked much about what brought her to the Southeastern Shipyards or about finances, so Jessie was a little surprised at her reaction.

CHAPTER 25

When Jessie returned home from work on Friday, she was surprised that she had received a letter. At first she thought it was from Al, but as soon as she saw the handwriting she realized it was not. It was, however, from a serviceman, and it took her a moment to realize who it was from. Owen Doi. She ripped it open and read it quickly.

Dear Jessie,

I guess you will be surprised to hear from me, but I needed to write to you because you were so kind to me at a time when few others were. I will never forget that. After you left, I felt bad about not thanking you for standing up for me at school. Anyway, a lot has happened in my life since I saw you.

First of all, my family and I moved to Arizona not long after you left Alabama because there were some Japanese-Americans there who were friends of my parents. That sounded like a good idea, but it may have led to my family being sent to an internment camp not far from Phoenix. At least my mother felt like we might have been better off staying in Alabama. But that's in the past.

Anyway, after a few months my brother and I were allowed to join the Army and fight for the United States, for which I am extremely proud. Eventually my parents were released and allowed to leave. They are now back in Alabama. I contacted my mother a few weeks ago, and she was able to get your address from your Aunt Lexie.

I have been stationed in Italy since the last of March. You may have heard on the news about the Po Valley Campaign. That's where I've been. It was a tough battle. The mountainous terrain made it difficult. We often had to crawl on our hands and knees for miles to get to our destination. The fighting lasted all of the month of April, but we beat them and it was over on May 2 in Italy. I was in Genoa when we heard about the Germans surrendering to the Allies in France the other day.

I will probably be going back home to Alabama soon, as they have told the 442nd Regiment that we will not be allowed to fight in the war against Japan. They say we look too much like them!

Again, I wanted to thank you for your friendship in the spring of 1942, when I had so few who would even speak to me. I have thought about your words of encouragement often over the last few years.

Your friend,
Owen

Jessie refolded the letter, laid it on her bedside table, and smiled. Her mind went back to the days in the spring of 1942 when she was so concerned about her friend Owen. He had made it! He had proved that he was a loyal American. She would call her Aunt Lexie and get his parents' address. She would write him a letter so that it would be there when he returned to Alabama. Who knows? She might even be back in Alabama too by that time—but probably not.

As the summer rolled along, Jessie and Linda attended ballgames, movies, and even went to Hunter Air Base and danced with the soldiers a few times, but they were beginning to think that the war might be coming to a close. Some of the talk was about the shipbuilding slowing down, which it was, but much of the news was about the new president.

At work, employees were conflicted. On one hand they looked forward to the ending of the war. But on the other hand, many were concerned about their jobs. This was especially true for the women. Sam came to lunch one day with a somber expression on her face. When she sat down and opened her lunch, she burst into tears. Jessie had never seen her so distraught.

"What is it?" asked Jessie, predicting the answer.

"This is my last week to work here. I told you I would be one of the first to go."

"But don't you need to go back to school, like I do?"

"Yes, I do," said Sam. "But you don't have the same situation that I do. I have to earn my money before I can even think of going to school."

"Maybe you can talk to the superintendent or something. Maybe they'll let you stay on, or maybe you could talk to someone at your school who could help you with getting a scholarship. There's got to be a way for you to go to school."

"That's the trouble with you white people. You don't see the problem because you don't have to deal with the things we do. You just ask and receive. You just explain the problem and get help. It's not that way with me."

"I actually have problems too, Sam. I don't know who's going to pay for my schooling either. I'm hoping that my father might help some, but he may not. I may have to work and save for my tuition. I may not be able to get a scholarship. But I'm willing to fight for it. And I'm willing to fight for you too. We'll work on it together."

"I'm sorry," apologized Sam. "You're right. I'm not the only one who has problems, but I thought I'd be working at least through December. The thing that bothered me most was that I am the only one on our crew who is being cut. Of course, all the rest of you are welders. But that's because you're white. I think I could learn how to weld. But I wasn't allowed to because of my skin color."

"I know. It's not fair. Did you know that I recommended that they let you train to be a welder?"

Sam laughed. "No. What did they say?"

"The same thing you said—you're not the right color," said Jessie, laughing.

"Well, I feel better now anyway!" said Sam.

"I have an idea," said Jessie. "You and I are both smart, and I think that even though we haven't been in school, we've probably learned as much during the time we've been here as the ones who stayed in school, don't you?"

"I've probably learned more," said Sam. "My school isn't that great."

"I heard that there is some kind of test you can take to get a diploma when you can't go to school. Why don't we go back to our schools and ask if we can take the test for graduation and see if we can pass it? If we can, then we can go on and get ready for college, even if we have to work a year. If we can't, we can still go back to school."

After work that day, Jessie went to see the supervisor of Slab #6. He seemed surprised when she entered his office. "Well, what have you come to complain about, little girl? Having to work too hard?"

"Actually, no. I'm fine. I wanted to speak with you on behalf of the black girl who works on our slab, Samantha. I understand that she's being cut after this week."

"Yes, she is. You probably don't need to be talking to her. It doesn't look good. As a matter of fact, I seem to remember advising you to keep away from the black employees."

"Skin color isn't all there is to a person, you know," said Jessie.

"Of course not. Some black people are hard-working, and some are lazy. I know that."

"Sam is hard-working, and she's also very smart. Do you know what she wants to be?"

"No."

"Sam lost her mother to cancer when she was ten years old, and she wants to become a doctor and help people like her mother."

"So what's this got to do with your visit to my office?"

"I want to make one simple request. I want Sam to be able to work until the rest of the crew is cut." Jessie looked the man straight in the eye as she made her request.

Jessie's supervisor sat there for a moment, looking as if he was having conflicting thoughts about whether to grant her request. Finally, he said, "I may get in trouble for this, but I'll see if I can convince my boss to let her stay."

"Thank you," said Jessie as she stood up.

"What did you say to the supervisor?" asked Sam the next day.

Jessie smiled. "Nothing much. I just asked if you could stay on until the rest of the crew had to leave."

"You must have said the magic word, because he told me I could continue," said Sam. "Thank you."

After that, most days at lunch Sam and Jessie talked about their future school plans. One day Jessie said, "I think I've figured out how we can avoid spending an extra year in high school. My mama said I was right. They do have a test we can take. It's a General Equivalency test to determine what you know. She says it's mostly for soldiers coming home, but they may allow those of us who have worked on the home front to take it in some circumstances. Anyway, she will check into it."

"But what if we can't pass it—or me anyway. You probably can."

"Well, if you don't pass it the first time, you could probably study a few weeks and pass. I think you could anyway. It would be better than spending a whole year in school. It's worth a try, don't you think?" said Jessie.

"Definitely. Let me know what your mother finds out."

CHAPTER 26

In June and July of 1945 most of the war news focused on what was going on in and around Japan. Jessie and her mother kept a close eye on their map each night, trying to identify the tiny islands.

Since the first of April, fighting had continued in Okinawa. The United States had suffered heavy losses, and the Japanese had lost even more. Finally, on June 22, the Allied forces won the battle. American Gen. Simon B. Buckner was killed by artillery fire, and Japanese Gen. Ushijima Mitsuru committed suicide. Also, many civilians in Okinawa committed suicide at the command of the military, according to reports.

With the signing of the charter of the United Nations in June, there was some hope for peace. At the same time, though, tensions were still high with the Japanese, so there was no conclusion to the war. And there was job uncertainty for many at Southeastern.

Mixed in with the news of war results were comments regarding President Truman and his opinions about Soviet Russia. It was a time of uncertainty. According to the president, he had received very little briefing on many of the unfolding problems with Russia. When President Roosevelt died unexpectedly, Truman told reporters, "I felt like the moon, the stars, and all the planets had fallen on me."

On July 16 the news reporter disclosed, "Today an unknown blast shook the desolate New Mexico desert, according to the residents of the village of Tularosa. The Army officials there said it was an ammunition explosion of some sort."

The next day at work, Jessie heard some talk about the explosion in New Mexico. "Do you think that blast was some kind of bomb they're testing?" asked one of her coworkers.

"Probably. We may all be blown up before it's over," commented another. Another reason to fear, thought Jessie. Jessie did not consider herself a worrier, but what else could one do? When would she be able to be a normal teenager, enjoying school?

It wasn't long before Jessie and her coworkers knew what the explosion in New Mexico was all about. On the morning of August 6, at about 10:45, President Truman announced that an American plane had dropped the single atomic bomb on the Japanese city of Hiroshima, an important military center. Jessie and her mother first heard the news at work, and learned more details on the evening news.

The War Department described the effects of the bomb by describing the results of the test in New Mexico. They said a huge steel tower had been "vaporized" by the explosion and people had been knocked down 10,000 yards away. President Truman warned the Japanese that if they did not accept the terms of the Potsdam Declaration, they could expect a "rain of ruin from the air."

The news sent chills up and down Jessie's spine. The descriptions of the bomb were full of mystery. Reports did not indicate how large the bomb was or what kind of plane dropped it or whether there were plans to make more bombs. She preferred not to think about it, but it was there all around her. People talked about it all the next day.

"Did you hear that the bomb possessed more power than 20,000 tons of TNT?"

"They've been working on it since 1939, and the British and Canadians are in on it. How come no one knew about it?"

"I don't know. They said that to date, America has spent nearly two billion dollars in advancing research on it."

"Two billion dollars? I can't even imagine that."

On August 9, news came of a bomb being dropped in a place called Nagasaki. The War Department had code names for these bombs: this one was called "Fat Man," and the one on Hiroshima "Little Boy." Jessie imagined what it would look like in a place where these powerful bombs had been dropped. She had seen pictures of places in London that had been bombed, and the atomic bombs were supposed to be much more destructive.

By the end of the day, Jessie was wanting to put her hands over her ears so she could not hear all the talk about the bomb. She curled up in her bed that night, hoping to sleep, but she kept hearing the voices of the newsmen and her coworkers talking about "the bomb." When she finally went to sleep, she dreamed that she heard a giant explosion and then went outside and saw a little thing about the size of a baseball that had enormous power. A little fat man held it in his hand and pulled it back as if he were going to throw it at her. She awoke in a panic.

The tension was palpable the first few days after that second bomb was dropped. "What will they do next? Drop a bomb on Tokyo? I heard they might," said one of Jessie's friends.

Southeastern had cut back on production, so Jessie had been working on the inner bottom of a ship instead of her customary site. She had not seen Sam for several days and had wondered if she was still working, but one day Sam showed up at the place where they usually ate lunch.

"Where have you been?" asked Jessie.

"I have been working on the fore peak of a ship, but today is my last day," said Sam. "It's over for me."

"I'm sorry," said Jessie. "But it's probably over for me in a few days too."

"Where are you working?"

"I've been welding on the inner bottom of that ship over there," said Jessie, pointing toward one of the ships. "It's awful in there. I never thought I was claustrophobic, but I'm beginning to think so."

"It's that bad, huh?" asked Sam.

"Yes! I have to crawl back in there. There's not room to stand up, and it's so dark I have to carry a light. Half the time when I get back in there I find that the temperature of the rod isn't right, and I have to pull the hose all the way back outside to the machine and reset the heat on the rod."

"That sounds awful," said Sam.

"And then there's the August heat and all the noise. It's the worst possible thing to do, I think." Jessie shook her head. "Well, I guess it's my patriotic duty, along with buying war bonds and all the other stuff."

"I heard the other day that one girl got attacked while working in the inner bottom of one of the ships. Aren't you afraid?"

"No one has bothered me. I haven't thought much about it. I've heard those stories, but there's really nothing I can do except continue my job," responded Jessie. "Maybe I should be afraid, but I haven't been."

"By the way," said Sam. "Have you heard any more about those tests we can take to graduate from high school?"

"Oh, yes. My mama got the address of the place where we can go check it out. I have it in a pocket somewhere." Jessie looked in two pockets and finally pulled out a crumpled piece of paper with some information written on it. "I hope you can still read it. I've been carrying it with me for three days, hoping to see you." She handed it to Sam.

"I wonder if they'll even consider letting me take the test," said Sam.

"Mama said to tell you to get one of your teachers to write you a letter of recommendation. That might increase your chances of being considered. If I were you, I would try to get a science teacher to do it, since that is your strongest subject."

"That's a good idea," agreed Sam. "I would not have thought to do it."

"Mama has decided to stay on in Savannah and work. In fact, she's already got a job at Adler's Department Store down on Broughton Street. She starts there on Monday. She didn't want to wait until they let her go at the shipyard before looking for another job."

"Will you stay in Savannah too?" asked Sam.

"I'm not sure. I guess it depends on whether they let me take that test or not. If they let me take it, and I pass, I may stay with Mama until I go to college. If not, I may go back to Alabama and stay with my grandmother for my final year of high school."

Not knowing what would happen in the next few days, the two girls exchanged phone numbers when they left lunch that day so they could stay in touch. And they did not see each other again at the shipyards.

One morning in the middle of August there was talk that the Japanese had surrendered. About the middle of the morning, word spread that all employees were to meet at noon for a special announcement. The shipyard was all buzzing with speculation about the announcement. Had they dropped another bomb, or had Japan surrendered to the Allies?

When Jessie came out at noon for the meeting, she saw that they had set up a public address system. When she saw it, she knew this was a big deal. They usually only had the loud speaker at the ship launchings. There was a huge crowd gathered. It looked like all six thousand employees that were left at work had gathered.

As soon as the clock struck twelve noon, Jessie saw one of the head men of the shipyard approach the microphone. The crowd quieted. "I am sure some of you heard President Truman's announcement that the Japanese government has given a full acceptance of the Potsdam Declaration that specifies the unconditional surrender of Japan. Although the official papers will be signed later, this is to inform you that the war is over!"

A shout of exclamation went up immediately.

"Just a minute," said the speaker. "Before we get too loud, I want us to take a moment to express gratitude to God for this momentous occasion. I have asked Mr. Grant to say a prayer of thanksgiving. Would all of you gentlemen please remove your hats as Mr. Grant comes to express thanks?" Hundreds of men took off their hats and bowed their heads as Mr. Grant came to the microphone. After the prayer the crowd began to disperse back to their work sites, and all seemed to return to normal—except it wasn't, of course. The war was over!

That evening Bernadette and Jessie visited with the Johnsons, and all the conversation centered around the Japanese surrender.

"Were you all at the shipyard when it was announced?" asked Chad.

"Yes, along with all the thousands of other workers," said Bernadette.

"I wasn't there. One of my workers got hurt, and I had to drive him downtown to get stitches. It was total chaos down there. I didn't go into the shopping area of Broughton Street, but it was crazy. Everyone seemed to have gathered there. You could hear car horns, church bells, sirens, and shouting and yelling on the street. The police had to block off some of the traffic because of all the people in the middle of the street."

"Do you think they will just lay everyone off in the next few days?" Jessie asked Chad.

"I don't know, but I think they'll be winding things down soon. They may do it gradually. I hope they will continue building other kinds of ships, but I know it won't require the number of workers we've had the last few years."

In the coming days employees learned that as they finished the projects they were working on, many of them would no longer be needed. After Bernadette started working at Adler's Department Store, she told Jessie to apply to take the General Equivalency test for a high school diploma. She learned that they would give it again in two weeks.

"Should I take it that soon?" she asked Linda. "Maybe I need to study for a few weeks before doing it. What if I fail?"

"When do you want to start college?" asked Linda. "Is it possible you can get into college in January? If so, you may want to take the test now. You can't apply to college without a high school diploma."

"That's true. Well, I'll never know until I try. I'll go ahead and sign up to take the test in two weeks."

"How much longer will you be working?" inquired Linda.

"Just until the end of the week. And I'm glad. No more crawling around in the bottom of that ship! What about you?"

"I'll be finished at the end of the week too. I've been offered a job at the school where Mary will go next fall. It's close to her daycare, so I will be able to drop her off on my way to and from work for the next few months," said Linda. "I'm really excited. I hope to enroll in college and get a teaching degree eventually."

"I thought you said you wanted to be a nurse," said Jessie.

"I did. Over the last few months, though, I've been doing a lot of thinking. I guess that since I married a doctor, I just naturally thought I'd like to be in the medical field. Lately I have realized that I really love working with children. It's funny how you can let someone else influence your identity. I have realized that science and medicine just aren't what I enjoy."

"I think you'll be a good teacher," affirmed Jessie. "I just remembered that time you mentioned being a nurse."

"You know what made me realize I wanted to be a teacher?"

"What?"

"Your little cousins. When I kept Carol and the twins, I loved having them, along with Mary. Having John and Mack, along with Carol and Mary, was fun for me. I began to think that I would love being around children all day."

"That's great. When will you start college?"

"I don't know," said Linda. "I'll work at the school as the receptionist for a while, get to know how the school operates, and everything. Then I'll talk to them about my desire to go back to school. I'm not in a big hurry. But at some point I hope to continue my education."

Jessie smiled. "We women—we can do it! I know you'll make it. Men aren't the only ones who can make a living!"

"That's one thing I've learned at Southeastern. When I was married, I felt so dependent on my husband. I think he encouraged that feeling. He would say, 'You have it made. You don't have to work.' He was right, of course. Somehow it always made me feel incompetent though. I do have it harder in some ways now, but I think I'm happier."

"I don't think my mother has ever got to the point where she could move on like that with her life. I think she is still bitter about my father leaving us. Did I tell you that he came to Cornelia's funeral?"

"No. What did he say? Or do?"

"He didn't say much, and I was so upset that I was really rude to him. I have written him a letter though. It was sort of an apology. I guess I acted kind of like my mother when he came. I was angry at everyone."

"That's understandable," said Linda. "But you showed a lot of maturity by writing to him to apologize."

"I'm not sure about that. I have very mixed feelings about my dad. He has never been around much, so I don't really know him. After he left the cemetery that day, I felt really bad about how I'd treated him. He seemed so sad, and I wanted to make it right." Jessie laughed. "But one of the reasons I wrote to him was that I am hoping he'll help with my college tuition. Is that bad?"

"No. He *should* help with your college expenses. He's your father."

"I know. But after the way I treated him, it just seems that he may think it's not a sincere apology."

"No matter what he thinks, he left you as a young child. It was wrong for him not to keep in touch, so there was good reason for you to feel anger when he appeared at your sister's funeral. That does not mean that he has any reason not to help you with college."

"Well, I hope he sees it that way," said Jessie. "I am just not sure how I'll pay for college if he cannot, or does not want to, pay for my tuition. I've saved up a little money from working, and I've bought a lot of war bonds, but they won't pay for all my expenses."

CHAPTER 27

When Jessie went to the office to inquire about the test she needed to take for her high school diploma, she approached a desk with a nameplate that read "Mrs. Jones" on it and a middle-aged lady sitting behind it. When Jessie told her she was there to ask about the General Equivalency test, the lady seemed surprised.

"This is a program mainly for returning soldiers," Mrs. Jones said. "You don't seem to fit that category."

Jessie explained that she had been working at the shipyards for two years and still lacked a year of high school.

"Well, I guess you could take it then. Did you bring the transcript from your high school? We'll need that to determine if you are eligible." Jessie shook her head.

"I didn't know I had to have it. I can get it though."

"Where did you go to school? Here in Savannah?"

"No. I lived in Alabama."

"That presents a bit of a problem. Alabama schools don't require as much math as we do here in Savannah, and the test has some tough math questions on it. Why don't you wait until the next time it is given and study up on your math? We can give you some material to study," said the lady, handing her the address to give the school for mailing a transcript.

Looking at Jessie's face, the lady smiled. "I know this is a disappointment, but if you take the test next week and fail that part, it will take you even longer to get your diploma. Also, we need your transcript before we let you take the test, so we might not even be able to let you take it at the next administration of the test anyway if your school doesn't send it immediately."

Jessie wondered if Sam even stood a chance at getting to take the test. "Could I ask you something?" she inquired.

"Sure. What is it?" asked the lady at the desk.

"Do any black students ever take this test?"

The lady raised her eyebrows and looked shocked. "Not that I know of. Why?"

"I just wondered. Would there be any reason they couldn't?"

"None that I can think of, but I doubt they could pass it."

"But if they could pass it, they could get a diploma, right?"

"I suppose so."

"Thank you," said Jessie, gathering up her things. "Did you say you had some math materials I could take with me and study?"

"Yes. You will need to sign for them, though, and bring them back before you are allowed to take the test." The lady then brought out the little booklet and had Jessie sign a statement saying that she would be responsible for returning it before taking the test.

The next day Jessie called her school and asked the office personnel to send her transcript to the lady in Savannah, then she began immediately to study the math in the little booklet. She was glad she had not signed up to take the test this time, as she had not studied that material before. The days and weeks passed quickly, then Jessie was ready to take the test.

On the appointed day she walked into the testing room with her head held high. She sat down near the front of the room. There were several young men (obviously returning soldiers) in the room and one older lady who looked to be about middle age. As Jessie scanned the room, she saw an open door to the side. At first she assumed the room was empty, then she saw a slight movement and realized someone was in there. It was Sam! She smiled and went back to the test questions.

Throughout September and October, Jessie waited for a response from her father. She had told her mother that she had written him, but had not told her any of the letter's contents. She was glad her mother did not press for details. She wasn't sure what her mother would think about either her apology or her request for help with college. She suspected that if he was not willing to help her, her mother's response would be an "I told you so" lecture. Jessie had also written to request an application from George Washington University but had not yet received the application. She thought she could go ahead and fill out the application but not mail it until she received her diploma—*if* she got one!

On the last Friday in October the postman delivered two letters for Jessie: one from her father and one from the General Equivalency test! Ripping open the test results first, she saw that she had passed with flying colors. Then she took more time opening the letter from her father.

Dear Jestina,

I'm sorry it has taken a few weeks to write this, but I've been trying to decide how to express my feelings. First of all, you didn't need to apologize for your actions. I am the one who has lots to apologize for. But I will tell you that I have never received a more welcome letter. The very fact that you are willing to write to me made me happy. As I am sure Bernadette has told you, I have made many mistakes. I have been painfully aware of them since we lost Cornelia. You were exactly right. My appearance at the funeral was too late. But maybe it's not too late for you.

I hope that I can in some way make it up to you a little by helping you with college expenses. Please call and let me know where you have applied and give me details about what you need. I'm not rich of course, but I am your father, and I want to help you.

Love,
Your Father, Dan Thompson

Jessie sat on her bed and cried for all the opportunities she and her dad had missed. She knew it was not her fault, but she wished that it could have been different. Maybe they could begin anew and have a different relationship.

She considered calling Sam to see if she had received her results, but thought it might be bad if Sam had not heard, so she put it off until the next week. She mailed her application on Monday. Then she waited. She was counting the days, trying to determine whether she would get accepted in time to begin college in January. She doubted it, but it was possible.

Throughout most of November, Jessie spent her days helping Linda when Mary was not at preschool and helping the Johnsons with the twins. The Monday before Thanksgiving, she heard the phone ringing as she opened the door at home.

"Hello," she said.

"Hello to you, my friend," said a slightly familiar voice. "Do you know who this is?"

"I'm not sure. Sam?" Jessie asked.

"Yes."

"How are you?"

"I'm fine. In fact, I'm great. I wanted to tell you that I've been accepted to the University of Illinois, and I'll be leaving in about two weeks," Sam said ecstatically.

"Oh, I am so excited for you!" Jessie practically yelled into the phone.

"I can't believe it! And I told you about my cousin who lives there. I talked to her, and she says I can stay with her. I will pay her a small fee, which will help her out. Well, she has found me a job where I can work part time and make the money to pay her. *And*, I got a scholarship to pay my tuition!"

"All that in just a few weeks? You have been busy!"

"What about you? Have you made progress too?"

"Yes. But not as much as you have. I did get my diploma—which obviously you did too. I saw you on test day, by the way. Anyway, I sent my application to George Washington University, but haven't heard back, so we'll see. But I did write my dad a letter, and he says he'll help me with expenses."

"Thank God for that," said Sam. "I'm sure you'll be accepted."

When she hung up, Jessie did a little dance around the room. Sam deserved this. She was an amazing young lady. So many people thought that because a person had a dark skin color they would never be successful, but Jessie had never met a person, girl or boy, who had both the intelligence and the motivation she had observed in Sam. *Even if I don't get into college in January, I'm glad Sam did,* thought Jessie.

By the middle of December, however, she was getting extremely anxious about her possibilities. Surely the university would let her know soon. The university classes did not begin until close to the end of January, so there was still time.

"Mama, even if I get accepted, I have no way to get to Washington," Jessie said one evening.

"Maybe you could see if Cassidy is coming back to visit her aunt during Christmas. Somebody would be taking her back to Washington, D.C. Maybe you could go over there and go with them," said her mother.

"I don't know. I'd hate to call them and then not be accepted. I'd be so embarrassed. Besides, I don't even know if Cassidy is still in Washington now. I haven't heard anything from her in a long time. And it's so far back to Alabama from here." Jessie sighed. "I'll just wait and see if I'm accepted and then worry about how I'll get to Washington."

"Have you heard any more from Dan? Maybe he'll help you," Bernadette said. She had not said much about Jessie's father's offer to help her, and Jessie suspected that her mother was doubtful he'd actually help.

"I got a letter last week. He told me to call him as soon as I heard that I was accepted and he would send a check. I haven't mentioned transportation," said Jessie. "I've saved up a little money. Do you know how much a bus ticket is?"

"No, but I will check. I have a little I could give you too." Bernadette went over and checked the drawer where she kept some money. She pulled out an envelope and looked at its contents and then replaced it. Jessie guessed she was checking to see how much she could afford to put in on a bus ticket before she called and asked about it.

The next afternoon Bernadette was still at work, so Jessie ran over to Linda's —waving a letter in one hand as she knocked on the door with the other. "Linda! Linda!" she shouted.

"What is it?" Linda said when she saw the smile on Jessie's face.

"I got accepted into George Washington University! It says right here," said Jessie, pointing to the letter. "I am to report on January 15 and will start classes the following week."

"Wonderful," said Linda. "And your dad is paying tuition for you?"

"Yes. All I need now is a bus ticket."

Chapter 28

That evening Jessie called her father and gave him the details of her acceptance. She would be able to work for some of her expenses, and she told him the exact amount he would have to pay. He did not hesitate to tell her that he would send a check immediately.

That weekend when Jessie and her mother went to the Johnsons' home to keep the kids for a while so their parents could go to a movie, they gave Chad and Pat the good news.

"That is wonderful! I know you were concerned, but I never had any doubt that you'd get accepted," said Chad.

"Me either," agreed Pat. "Now, what can we do to help? After all the free babysitting you've done for us, we want to do something for you."

Jessie looked at her mother. "You don't owe me anything, of course. The only thing I'm not sure about is how I'll get there. Mama and I are hoping we can scrape together enough money for a bus ticket, but we haven't had time to check on how much it will be yet. Depending on how much it is, maybe you could help us a little with that."

"Consider it done," said Chad. "Let the bus ticket be our gift to you."

When Jessie and her mother started to protest, Pat said, "No, we want to do this. We are so proud of you, and we want to do something to help."

Relieved of worry about the cost of a bus ticket, Jessie and her mother spent the next few weeks getting her ready to go to college. Jessie made lists of everything she had been told she would need—clothes, notebooks, pencils, and an assortment of other items. It had helped that Bernadette was working at Adler's because they were able to purchase most of her clothes there at a discount.

Finally the day arrived for her departure. Chad volunteered to drive Jessie and her mother to the Greyhound bus depot to see her off. Chad had picked up her ticket himself the day before.

"I'm glad you could take us," said Bernadette when they left early that morning. It was not quite daylight when they drove into Savannah. The city was still quiet. "Where is the Greyhound station?"

"It's 109 West Broad. It's easy to see once you get down there. I had no trouble finding it yesterday. They have a nice little diner in there. Maybe we can get a bite to eat before you leave, if there's time."

"That would be great. I brought a snack or two, but I would love to eat something before I go," Jessie said as they pulled into the parking area near the bus depot. Her stomach felt a little tight, like it was in a knot. "I've never traveled alone before," she said. "What do I do when I get to Washington? Will they tell me how to find a ride to the university?"

"Of course. Just ask someone where to find a cab if you don't see one," said Chad. "Cabs will probably be waiting around the station, but don't be afraid to ask. There'll probably be plenty of other college students coming in at the same time you are anyway, so they'll be used to questions about transportation to various colleges and universities in the area."

As they slipped into a seat near the lunch counter and ordered egg biscuits, Jessie realized that she was beginning a new era of her life. The last two years had been difficult, but she had not really chosen them. Her mother had. Now she was beginning a life she had chosen, a time of learning what she wanted to learn. But what did she want to learn?

She wasn't completely sure. She wanted to do something where she could help people, especially people who were treated unfairly—such as her friend Sam, and Owen, and others she had met who were subjects of prejudice and unfair practices. She thought she might want to be a lawyer, but she wasn't sure. Some women were becoming lawyers now, but they were often shunned by the law firms and not given partnerships.

"You're awfully quiet, Jessie," said her mother. "Are you all right?"

"Yes. I was just thinking about what I will study and learn at the university."

Soon it was time for them to gather up her luggage and get ready for her to board the bus.

"You'll have to write me and tell me all about your studies once you get started," said Bernadette. "I'll be missing you, so don't forget to write."

"I won't," said Jessie. "I'll write as soon as I get my schedule of classes. It may be a week or so. I don't know how it all works. I'm a little nervous. I hope I can do it."

"Of course you can," said Bernadette and Chad at the same time.

"You've always been an excellent student," said Bernadette. "Your scores on the equivalency test showed how smart you are too."

"I hope I can do it," Jessie said. She hugged both her mother and Chad before turning to board the bus with the crowd of other people. Fortunately, she found a seat near the front of the bus and settled down for the long ride. As the bus pulled out, she saw her mother wipe a tear from her face as Chad guided her back toward the car. Jessie choked back her own tears. She could do this, she reminded herself.

She pulled out her copy of *Anne of Green Gables*, her all-time favorite book. She had first read it when she was eleven years old, but recently she had started to read it again. Although she saw the events differently now, it was still a great book, and she identified with Anne in a different way. She was reading the part where Anne was talking to Marilla about Diana. When she read the line, "Kindred spirits are not so scarce as I used to think. It's splendid to find out there are so many of them in the world," Jessie immediately thought of her friends Al and Sam and Linda. She would never have thought that any of them would have been her best friends, but they were. She would miss them.

CHAPTER 29

By the time she arrived in Washington, D.C., Jessie was exhausted. Taking out her instructions for getting to the location indicated in her last letter, she hurriedly found a cab and gave the driver the address. He nodded and motioned to another girl and a young man, who apparently had also asked about going to the same location. They got in the cab too.

"Are you a student at George Washington University?" she asked the girl.

"I'm going to be," said the girl shyly. "And you?"

"Me too," said Jessie. "I'll be a freshman."

"I'm scared to death," said the girl. "I live in West Virginia, and I've never even been here before."

"Well, I have never been anywhere but Alabama and Georgia. I came form Savannah," said Jessie. "Maybe we can stick together. We're probably going to the same place."

The cab drive did not seem long in comparison to the long bus ride, and she and the other girl found their way to their dorm.

"What do you plan to major in, Miss Thompson?" asked her advisor the next day.

"I am not sure. I think I want to be a lawyer, but I just can't decide. Is there any way you can help me in deciding?" inquired Jessie.

The advisor smiled. "That's what I'm here for, young lady. Of course I can. The first thing we'll do is get you scheduled to take a test that gives us some ideas about what you are interested in and what your strengths are. Meanwhile, you can know that there are several undergraduate majors you could choose from that would be helpful in the field of law. You can choose a major and then by the time you have to apply for law school, maybe you will know whether that's for you or not."

After Jessie took the test a few days later, she was told that her strengths were in social studies and English. She was given a list of majors in each of those fields.

"Any major in either of those areas would be good background for going into the field of law," said her advisor. "People who can communicate well are especially well-prepared for courtroom practice. Also, people who know history, government, and civics are better prepared to practice law, so think about it for this semester, and then you can decide. You will be busy with core subjects this semester anyway."

Feeling encouraged about her possibilities, Jessie went into one of the student areas where there was a little sandwich shop and sat down to read over the list of majors. With her head buried in the papers in one hand, and a cup of coffee in the other hand, she didn't notice anyone nearby until she heard a familiar voice. "Hey there, Jessie. I heard you might be coming here sometime. Welcome!"

Jessie had to turn all the way around in her chair, being careful not to spill the coffee. There stood Cassidy, looking smug and confident as usual. Jessie's face lit up. "Oh my goodness! I am *so* glad to see you. I thought you might be here already, but I didn't dare hope for it. The last time I talked to your aunt, she said you were going to work for the government in some secret job that you couldn't talk about."

"That's true. You will not believe what I've been doing until last September! I guess I can talk a little about it now that the war is over, but it's true. You know what they told us? They said if we told anyone where we worked or talked about it at all, we would be killed! You know that slogan that was going around 'loose lips sink ships'?" Jessie nodded.

"Well, I guess they believed that, because we worked in this secret place with a twelve-foot-high fence with barbed wire on the top all the way around it. We had to show our badge with our picture on it as we entered the gate and again when we entered the building. There were two of us who rode the bus to within about four blocks of it. We had to walk up a hill to the workplace. One day on the bus someone asked us, "Where do you two go every day?"

"Before I could answer, a man sitting across from me said, 'They go to play golf.' I guess he rode the bus to make sure we didn't tell anything. I don't know."

"What did you do? Can you tell now?"

Cassidy smiled. "I don't guess it matters now, but you know, I've kept quiet about it so long, I don't guess I will ever be able to say much. Anyway, we were helping with code-breaking. You know I was always a whiz at math, and that was all I did every day. We did all these equations all day and passed them along to our supervisors, and somehow they were able to break the codes. Our job was to find the unknown. We put the results into three different categories. We didn't actually know what the messages were, but our work allowed our supervisors to figure it out."

"Wow! Your job was intriguing. And I was just welding pieces of metal together," said Jessie.

"It was. We were helping to decode top-secret Japanese messages. One time there was this ship that was supposed to have medical supplies going into Cuba. But we determined that it was loaded with ammunition. Sure enough, when military officials opened it up they found ammunition, not medical supplies."

Jessie was stunned as she listened to Cassidy. "I guess you were relieved when the Japanese surrendered last August."

"I certainly was! When we heard the news, some of my friends and I went down to Fourteenth and Pennsylvania where lots of people had gathered to celebrate. A bunch of soldiers and sailors were there, and everyone was singing and dancing and shouting. A streetcar came down that way, and the military guys said, 'This street belongs to the United States service personnel' and just picked that streetcar up and set it off the street!"

The two girls laughed as they caught up on other news in their lives. Cassidy had heard about Cornelia's death from her aunt, who had attended the service.

"I am so sorry. How in the world were you able to go back to work after that?" asked Cassidy.

"I don't know. It was all a blur for weeks. Gradually I began to get back to some kind of normal life, but to be honest, it's still hard for me to believe she's gone," said Jessie. "I depended on her much more than I realized. It helped that Linda, our next-door neighbor, befriended me. I sort of adopted her as my sister."

"Did she work at the shipyards too?"

"Yes. She is older and has a little girl. She is divorced, so she has her own difficulties, but she was a lot of help to me. After a while she and I started going out to dances and movies the way Cornelia and I had," said Jessie. "No one can replace Cornelia, but it helped to have another young person to talk to, and Mama often kept Mary for Linda when we'd go places."

"Did you find a special boyfriend at any of those dances?" asked Cassidy, smiling mischievously.

Jessie swallowed hard. "No," she said. She sat there for a moment quietly, and Cassidy waited. Finally, Jessie cleared her throat. "Well, actually I met a young man that I really liked. His name was Al."

Cassidy waited a moment and then said, "You said his name *was* Al. Did he get killed or something?"

"I think so," said Jessie. She could see Al's face and his bald head. She could hear his Bing Crosby voice. Holding back her tears, she said, "I don't know for sure. He flew those B-17 bombers all the time. It was a very dangerous job."

"Why do you think he was killed?" asked Cassidy.

"We were writing every week, and then nothing. I haven't heard from him in more than a year."

"Couldn't you call someone and ask?"

"I don't know. We didn't really have a romantic relationship. We were just good friends. It's hard to explain. I don't even know his folks' names or addresses. They live somewhere in Oklahoma. Once I met a childhood friend of his, but I don't even know his last name," said Jessie. "And I only saw him once."

"If I were you, I'd try to find out," said Cassidy.

"What if he just decided he didn't want to write anymore? I don't even know if our friendship was that important to him. I thought it was, but things have just felt so uncertain the last few years. Nothing seems for sure."

Cassidy said, "I know. I sometimes feel the same way. War does that to people."

"And what about you? Do you have a boyfriend?" asked Jessie.

"Yes. As a matter of fact, I do. I met a soldier while I was working for the government. He was a medic in the Pacific. He was in D.C., and we went out a few times. I just knew he was the one, and fortunately he felt the same way. We began writing. Last summer he was injured while helping a wounded soldier and was in the hospital for a long time. When I get through college and he gets out of the service, though, we will get married. Or at least I hope so."

"That is wonderful! By the way, what are you studying here?"

"I really like math, so I've started with that. My advisor gave me several possibilities. She first said that I should plan to teach math, but I'm not sure I want to do that. Anyway, she said that this year I could just focus on core subjects and explore different occupations where math is important. Another thing she said was business-related—banking and things like that."

"I'm pretty sure I want to be a lawyer," said Jessie. "I am not sure of my undergraduate major though. Probably I'll choose English as a major, but I'd like to study some in the political sciences, government, and things like that."

"Great. I don't know any women lawyers," said Cassidy. "Maybe I can hire you if I ever need a lawyer!"

In the next few weeks Jessie and Cassidy saw each other several times, renewing their friendship and catching up on news from Jessie's hometown in Alabama. They did not have any classes together, but they met for lunch several times and went to dinner and a movie once or twice.

Jessie loved being at George Washington University, and she loved all her studies. She was being exposed to ideas and information she could not have imagined. She especially loved her history and English classes. Although she had never had to study so hard in her life, she loved every minute of it. Memorizing loads of information before every test, her grades demonstrated her acute interest in all the new information she was receiving. Some of her classmates were complaining about all the studying they had to do, but not Jessie. She loved it!

Toward the end of her first term, one of her English professors called her aside before class and asked her to come to his office that afternoon. The class required both composition skills and speaking skills. She had given two oral presentations and written several papers. She walked to the office, wondering if she had done something wrong. She had received high grades on all her assignments in his class. When she walked in, her prfessor was sitting behind his desk.

"Have a seat," he said. She sat down, fearing the worst. "I understand you are interested in law school after undergraduate studies."

"Yes, I hope to become a lawyer," she said.

"What makes you think you can be a lawyer? You know, not many women get accepted to law school. Even when they do get in, many drop out after a few terms. There are also a good many women lawyers who never get partnerships in firms. There's a lot of prejudice about women in the law profession."

"I am aware of that," said Jessie. "Are you saying that I should not become a lawyer?"

"No. Not really," said the professor. "I just want to be sure that you understand the struggles you'll have in law school and in the profession once you get into it."

"I think I do. I guess I can't know exactly until I get there, but I know what you're talking about. I really want to be a lawyer though."

"Why?"

"I want to help people who often don't get justice in our judicial system. I want to advocate for the underdog, so to speak."

The professor smiled. "You've got some rather noble goals set for yourself, haven't you? How did you get so mature at your age?"

"I spent two years working as a welder in the shipyards in Savannah, Georgia, before I came to college. I often saw people treated unfairly because they were women, or because they were black, or some other reason not based on their ability to do the job. I decided that I'd like to do something to help people who can't help themselves."

"I knew there was something different about you. I've been watching you this semester. You didn't seem like a typical first-year student. Now I understand why."

"I didn't know I was so different, but I have noticed that my perspective is not like that of most of the other students. I thought it was because I love school and have been waiting for two years to get away from the hard work of welding and back into the classroom," said Jessie.

"The reason I asked you to come in is that I wanted to suggest that you apply for a student assistant's job in the admissions office. It requires someone with good communication skills, because you would take students on tours of the campus when they come to visit. You would have to become familiar with details regarding our programs, and you would need to be positive about the school. If you're interested, you can just go apply and tell them I sent you. I'm not sure what it pays, but I know it would help with your expenses."

"I'm certainly interested. I was afraid I'd done something wrong when you asked me to come in here," said Jessie with a smile.

"You've done something right," he assured her.

Jessie went over to the admissions office that afternoon, and by the next week she had been trained in her duties for the job. She loved introducing visiting students and their parents to the campus and the university's programs. She quickly learned about almost all the undergraduate majors and most of the graduate programs. She found it especially helpful to learn all about the undergraduate political science courses, as well as all about the law school.

The week Jessie was hired, another student, a junior named Luke, also began work there. She had hoped they would be friends, but after a few days she realized they probably would not.

"What do you do here?" Luke asked on his first day.

"Give tours to visitors to the campus and explain about the programs, things like that," she said.

"Really?" he said, with a smirk. "I can't believe they're letting a freshman *girl* do this job. Do you even know what the school offers?"

"Yes. I had to learn all that before I started work." Jessie gritted her teeth, but said no more.

"Well, now that I'm here, you probably won't have much to do," he said. "Maybe you can take care of the clerical-type stuff while I show people around. I'm sure there'll be other things you can do."

"We'll see," she said. Now that she was away from home, she paid more attention to what her mother had tried to teach her. She kept hearing her mother's voice saying, "Watch what you say. You can get in trouble." She had grown up a little, and had gained a bit of confidence. Luke's opinion wasn't that important to her. She turned and walked out of the room without saying anything in response to his comments.

In the coming weeks she learned that visitors were often given a choice of the two student workers unless one was unavailable. When visitors came into her office, the counselor would tell them a little about the tour guides and ask them which one they preferred. She noticed that male students did often choose Luke, but most of the time the female visitors chose her. She was pleased to note that there was no real difference in the number of tours they gave. She also noted that Luke often had to come back and ask the admissions counselor questions that he should have known the answers to. One day she was in the lobby when he returned with his visitors. The counselor was in the lobby.

Jessie heard Luke ask a question about majors in one of the fields. The answer seemed simple to her. The counselor turned to her. "Jessie, could you help this young man?" She then proceeded to ask Jessie the young man's question, and Jessie answered it without hesitation.

Luke walked off, looking embarrassed. "I should have asked for you," the young man said, smiling at her. "That guy doesn't seem to know much about the university's programs at all."

Despite her frustrations with Luke, Jessie couldn't help feeling bad for him as he walked down the hall. Of course he brought it on himself. He was too self-assured and didn't work hard to learn all about the school. He had thought that because he was an upperclassman, and a male, he would naturally do a better job.

She smiled. "Well, I guess we all have our strengths and weaknesses," she said. After that day, Luke didn't say much to Jessie.

CHAPTER 30

As winter turned into spring, Jessie often thought of Al Donaldson and wondered if she would ever see him again. She tried to think of a way she could find out if he had survived the war, but all her ideas seemed childish, and she kept going back to the idea that maybe he just lost interest in her. Despite the dangerous nature of his job, she didn't believe he had died in the war. If he wanted to contact her, he could get in touch with her mother, because she had kept the same phone number when she moved to another house in Savannah. Every time she called her mother she would say, "Have I received any calls or letters?"

The answer would always be, "No." She tried to convince herself that it didn't matter, but she couldn't quite get Al out of her mind. Cassidy often suggested that she should forget about him and find some nice young man on campus and go out with him.

"But *you* are waiting for your soldier to come back and marry you," Jessie would say.

The fact was that Jessie had very little time for a social life. With classes and work during the day and studying at night, she had little spare time during the week, and she was exhausted on the weekends and usually had additional classwork to do.

With each month she realized she was more often thinking of herself as Jestina instead of Jessie. Her professors had her full name on their lists, so they always called her Jestina, and she never corrected them. She thought of her Aunt Lexie. She always called her niece Jestina, saying it was important that she remember what her name meant—just and upright. Gradually, since she had been in

Washington, she found that she was comfortable with her name and didn't expect to be called Jessie all the time.

One day she was reading in the commons area at GWU, absorbed in a novel she had to read for one of her classes. She had taken a cup of coffee with her and placed it on an adjoining table.

"Jessie!" She looked up to see Cassidy standing right across the table from her. She had not heard her come up.

"Cassidy, I didn't hear you come into the room," said Jessie.

"I called your name twice as I was walking up, before I *yelled* it," said Cassidy.

"I swear I did not hear a thing," said Jessie. "You know what I think the problem was?"

"You're going deaf?" asked Cassidy.

"I hope not. You are the only person here who calls me Jessie. Everyone else calls me Jestina. I must not be thinking of myself as Jessie now. Isn't that weird?"

"Yes, very weird," said Cassidy. "I guess if I want to get your attention, I'll have to start calling you Jestina too."

"No, you can keep calling me Jessie. You're the only one here who really knows me from when I was younger. I like that you're my long-time friend from Alabama. Besides, when I call my mama, she always calls me Jessie too."

"Okay, but I will say this: Jestina is a really good name for a lawyer—just and upright. Perfect!"

One day when Jessie dropped by the admissions office to see if she had any tours lined up that day, the admissions counselor said, "I was just about to call you. I had a young man come in this morning who wants you to give him a tour this afternoon. He came in and I knew your schedule was full, so I told him Luke was available, but when I told him that you would not be available until this afternoon, he said he'd come back later."

"Why did he want me instead of Luke?"

"I'm not sure. Maybe because I mentioned that you wanted to be a lawyer. He said he wanted to study law too. He seemed a little nervous about the whole idea of going back to school. He said he had been a prisoner of war in Germany for a while, and that he might decide to wait another year to apply, but wanted to see what it was like."

Many of their visitors these days were servicemen going back to school, and many of them had injuries of some kind, either physical or mental. Although she loved giving tours to those soldiers, they often chose Luke. "Okay. What time?"

"Two o'clock," the counselor said.

She smiled to herself. She always liked it when a male visitor specifically wanted her to do the tour, especially when Luke was available, but she would never say that to anyone.

"I'll be back at two then," she said.

She didn't get out of her class until after one, and there was a long line at the lunch counter. By the time she left the cafeteria it was almost two, and she had to retrieve her notes for the tour. She hated to rush into giving a tour. She always thought it made her seem disorganized and incompetent. She practically ran to the admissions office. Outside the door she stopped, took a deep breath, and tried to calm her thoughts before she entered. Then she put a smile on her face and opened the door. She stood face to face with a smiling young man— Al Donaldson!

SELECTED BIBLIOGRAPHY

Books

Baptist Hymnal, The. Nashville: Convention Press, 1991.

Colman, Penny. *Rosie the Riveter: Women Working on the Home Front in World War II.* New York: Yearling, 1998.

Cope, Tony. *On the Swing Shift: Building Liberty Ships in Savannah.* Annapolis, MD: Naval Institute Press, 2009.

Kiernan, Denise. *The Girls of Atomic City: The Untold Story of the Women Who Helped Win World War II.* New York: Touchstone, 2013.

Reid, Constance Bowman. *Slacks and Calluses: Our Summer in a Bomber Factory.* Washington, DC: Smithsonian Books, 1999.

Yellin, Emily. *Our Mothers' War: American Women at Home and at the Front During World War II.* New York: Free Press, 2004.

Electronic Material

Arlington National Cemetery, "Henry Louis Larsen, Lieutenant General, U.S. Marine Corps." http://www.arlingtoncemetery.net/hllarsen.htm.

"B-17 Bomber." http://www.history.com/topics/world-war-ii/world-war-ii-history/videos/boeing-b-17-flying-fortress-bomber.

"B-17 Flying Fortress." https://ww2db.com/aircraft_spec.php?aircraft_model_id=4.

"Battle of the Bulge." http://www.history.army.mil/html/reference/bulge/index.html.

"Battle of the Bulge." http://www.historynet.com/battle-of-the-bulge.

"Battle of Okinawa." http://www.history.com/topics/world-war-ii/battle-of-okinawa.

Burns, Ken, and Lynn Novick, directors. *The War,* http://www.pbs.org/thewar/about_letter_from_producers.htm.

Cowley, Robert, and Geoffrey Parker, eds. "Battle of the Bulge." http://www.history.com/topics/world-war-ii/battle-of-the-bulge.

Death of Hitler. http://www.history.com/topics/world-war-ii/adolf-hitler/videos/death-of-hitler.

"FDR Dies." *This Day in History*, http://www.history.com/this-day-in-history/fdr-dies.

Gantter, Raymond. *Roll Me Over: An Infantryman's WWII*, http://ww2today.com/25-december-1944-a-frozen-christmas-day-in-the-battle-of-the-bulge.

"George Washington University." https://politicalscience.columbian.gwu.edu/history-department.

"Georgia Greyhound Bus Stations." http://www.roadarch.com/bus/ga.html.

Hall, Michelle. "By the Numbers: World War II's Atomic Bombs." CNN Library, http://www.cnn.com/2013/08/06/world/asia/btn-atomic-bombs/index.html.

"History of the GED Test." https://www.gedtestingservice.com/testers/history.

"History of Public Education in Georgia." https://archives.columbusstate.edu/gah/1991/01-17.pdf.

Legacy Series, http://historymuseum.kennesaw.edu/. (Interviews with veterans, Rosies, Japanese Internment Camp residents, etc.)

Montgomery, L. M. *Anne of Green Gables, 1908.* https://www.goodreads.com/work/quotes/3464264-anne-of-green-gables.

Palomo, Tony, and Katherine Aguon. http://guamwarsurvivorstory.com/.

Shalett, Sidney. *The New York Times.* Aug. 6, 1945. http://www.nytimes.com/learning/general/onthisday/big/0806.html.

"The Ardennes Counteroffensive." *American Military History*, http://www.history.army.mil/books/AMH-V2/AMH%20V2/chapter5.htm#b10.

"The Death of President Franklin Roosevelt, 1945." *Eye Witness to History*, www.eyewitness-tohistory.com.

"United States Conducts First Test of the Atomic Bomb." http://www.history.com/this-day-in-history/united-states-conducts-first-test-of-the-atomic-bomb.

Miscellaneous

Girl Scout Leader. June 1944.

Jordan, Lou. 2012-2017. Interviews by author.

Tucker, Jane. 2012-2018. Interviews by author.

CPSIA information can be obtained
at www.ICGtesting.com
Printed in the USA
LVOW03s0313120118
562777LV00007B/8/P

9 781635 280388